Me, California Perkins *

by Patricia Beatty

Bonanza Girl
The Nickel-Plated Beauty
The Queen's Own Grove
Squaw Dog
published by William Morrow and Company

Indian Canoe-Maker
published by The Caxton Printers, Ltd.

The Lady from Black Hawk
published by McGraw-Hill Book Company

by John and Patricia Beatty

The Royal Dirk
Witch Dog
published by William Morrow and Company

At the Seven Stars
Campion Towers
A Donkey for the King
The Queen's Wizard
published by The Macmillan Company

Me, California Perkins

Patricia Beatty

illustrated by Liz Dauber

William Morrow & Company New York

To the Schlundt family,
Christena, Ellen, Carolyn,
and to my daughter, Ann.

✳ Contents

Me, California Perkins *

1 ✳ Something Drastic

The first thing Mama said when she saw our new home was, "Hiram Perkins! This is the Creator's dumping ground!"

She was talking about Mojaveville, "the boomiest boom city in the whole great sovereign state of California in 1882." Or at least that's what Uncle Hiram, Pa's youngest brother, had called it. He was the one who brought us out to Mojaveville. He was the "perpetrator of the awful deed" in Mama's later words.

This is what his letter that had come to us in Sacramento had said—the letter that was dated "sometime in April, maybe, or is it May yet?"

Dear folks, and this means all of you— Grandpa Thompson, my old carrot-top sister-in-law, Hope, and Oregon, Washington, and California, and you, my brother Gideon—all of you Sacramento Perkins folk.

Well, I cut loose out of Bodie last winter. There wasn't anything much doing there anymore so I come here to Mojaveville. Gideon, ain't you had enough yet of Sacramento? This place I'm at now is a real boomer—the boomiest boom city in the whole great sovereign state of California in 1882. We got us a silver strike here—horn silver you can pick up out of the ground—a real Eldorado.

You get yourselves packed up, you hear, and come down here and get rich. Don't you go telling me again, Hope, that Gideon ain't a miner. I know it. He's a carpenter, but Mojaveville needs carpenters bad—worse'n miners even maybe.

Get yourselves to a jumping off place by the

name of Burdoo. Then you can get a wagon from there or maybe even a stagecoach by the time you slowpokes get here. Come on, don't be sticks-in-the-mud. Head down here to the tall timber fast as you can and strike it rich.

The letter was signed "Hiram Perkins, with love." Underneath his name was a bunch of X marks for kisses. And there was a P.S. It wasn't Uncle Hiram's usual P.S., though. This one was short. His P.S.'s were longer than his letters most of the time. It said, "Bring Philip Atterbury with you. Everybody here likes yellow-spotted mutts. Ask for me at the Lion's Den when you get here. That's where I'll be."

"The Lion's Den!" Mama had exclaimed. She'd gone on ironing when Grandpa'd brought the letter into the house and read it out loud to us because Mama refused to open it at all. "What do you suppose that would be, Father?"

"Search me, honey." Grandpa, who was also a straight-nosed Thompson redhead like Mama and me, always called Mama, his only daughter, honey. Sometimes he called us that, too,—not all of the time, though. Grandpa was a cusser. "Maybe it's a hotel."

"Well, it is rather odd, isn't it?" Mama had sighed

and plunked the sadiron back onto its holder on the top of the stove. "What do you suppose Gideon will think of this latest letter?"

Grandpa had laughed at her. "Oh, Gid? He'll be rarin' to go."

"Pa rares easy when it comes to goin' places," put in my little brother, Washington, who was something of a "rarer" himself. That was because he had more Perkins blood than Thompson, and he was brown-haired, pointy-nosed like Orrie and Pa were, too.

"*That* Gideon does!" said Mama, who pursed the corners of her mouth the way she always did when the subject of Pa's itchy foot came up. She gave Wash a frosty blue-eyed stare that should have stopped a bear in its tracks, then she looked at Oregon and at me, California. "Callie," she said, "and you, too, Orrie, remember what I always told you. Never marry a man who has an itchy foot."

"You told us, too, never to marry a gambler," Orrie commented, nodding her head.

"There's a long list 'a men Mama says girls oughtn't to get married to," Wash said to Grandpa Thompson. Sometimes Wash and Pa and Grandpa were confederates, I thought, but I didn't dare tell them that. *Confederate* wasn't a word we spoke out loud in our house—not when Grandpa was around.

He'd been in the Mexican War first, then the Union Army in the Civil War, and was a G.A.R. member in Sacramento.

We finished eating our lunch; Mama finished the Tuesday ironing and didn't say anything about Uncle Hiram's letter anymore. All of us, even Wash, understood clearly by the way Mama slammed down the sadirons that she wasn't in a mood to talk about it. I felt the same way. After all, I was almost thirteen. I could remember how life had been with us for a long time, and I'd heard Mama tell the ladies at our church what things had been like when she'd married Gideon Perkins back in 1867. They'd got worse and worse since then. My parents were married in San Francisco and then went to Idaho Territory and then to Utah Territory and then back to California, where I was born, then to Oregon, where Orrie was born two years after me, up to Washington Territory, where Wash arrived about a year later, back to Idaho, and finally on to California again—to Sacramento. Pa'd carpentered every single place. Each time they got settled in, Uncle Hiram had written a letter, telling him to "pack up and come on up—or down."

"It's all right for Hiram. He's a bachelor," I'd heard Mama complain many times to Pa. "Bachelors don't care much about how things are or how they

live. It didn't matter to Hiram that we half-froze to
death in Idaho Territory and got rained out up
north two times. It doesn't seem to matter to you
either, Gideon, if we all die of pneumonia—you a
married man with three children to educate."

Pa was a mildish sort of talker but all the same,
stubborn. He'd answer her, "Well, they seem to be
getting educated all right, don't they, Hope?"

"That's because we're here in Sacramento," Mama
told him. "Callie's gone to three different schools
already. That's too many. I want her to go through
high school. There's one here. She wants to be a
schoolteacher, you know that. She can't be a teacher
unless she goes to high school, Gideon. These un-
civilized places Hiram finds don't even have schools
half the time, and we have to start them. I'm tired of
starting schools."

Pa hadn't answered her. We all knew how Mama
had set her heart on being a teacher, but instead
had married him after two years of high school. Pa'd
only gone through the seventh grade, because he
didn't take to more learning and he didn't figure he
needed any more to be a carpenter. Uncle Hiram
had quit in the sixth grade because learning didn't
take to him, was what Mama told us.

* * *

She didn't mention the letter during dinner, but after dinner she brought it out from under the big cake plate, where she kept old bills and things we hadn't paid yet, and handed it across the table to Pa. I guessed she kept it back so she could enjoy our stewed chicken, too.

His eyes lit up the way they usually did when he saw his brother's handwriting. "It's from Hiram," he said, sounding happy.

"Yes, it's from Hiram," Mama told him.

"I see from the envelope he's in a new place—not in Bodie anymore," commented Pa.

Wash piped up now. "He's out in Mojaveville."

"Never heard tell of it, Wash," came from Pa.

"It's another new place Hiram found." These were Grandpa Thompson's words.

"Now if you folks'd just let me read the letter in peace," complained Pa.

We shut up and sat quiet so Pa could read, all except Mama, who went across the kitchen and began to pump the pump handle. I had a good look at her face when she got up from the table. There was a storm coming all right. I got up, too, and pushed my chair back. "I'm gonna' go outside, Mama. Call me when you want me. You know where I'll be when it's time to wipe the dishes."

"You do that, Callie," she said, thumping down a dirty platter on the sideboard.

Pa was busy with the letter yet, and Grandpa Thompson was drumming with his fingers on the tablecloth. Neither one of them was looking at me, so I crooked my finger at my sister and brother and pointed up at the ceiling. That meant something we all understood clear as a bell—"let's go up in our tree house." Pa'd built us one the summer before. It was the special place we went to get away from grownups. Sometimes we suffered from adults. It wasn't everybody in the neighborhood who had a tree house of his very own. That's what came of having a Pa who was a carpenter and of having a big old oak tree in the side of the yard.

We climbed up the ladder and sat down on the floor. The wind was blowing coolish so the tree was swaying just a little bit. It was really nice up there. Wash was the first one to say something, the thing we were all thinking. "I bet we're going to sell this house, too, and head for Mojaveville, wherever it is."

"Up in Uncle Hiram's tall timber?" asked Orrie, in a puzzled tone.

"Yep, Pa'll want to go there all right," I agreed. Then I added, "But I don't think it's gonna' work this time—Pa getting his way. Mama's sick and tired of moving around. She likes Sacramento."

"Want'a bet, Callie?" asked Wash.

I was wrong. That night while I wiped the dishes Mama told me we'd be leaving pretty soon, she thought.

"For Mojaveville?" I asked her.

"Yes." She didn't say anything more, but she went across the kitchen and touched the broom closet Pa had just made for her and then the cupboard for her best set of dishes, some more of Pa's carpentering work. I figured she was saying good-by to them. Mama loved our house in Sacramento. It had been big enough to begin with, but when Pa'd had "slow times" carpentering, he'd worked on it, fixing it up. It was almost the way Mama liked it by now.

I had to know if he'd said it again. "Did Pa say things were slow here in Sacramento, Mama?"

"Yes, Callie."

I knew what that meant all right. It was always his excuse for his itchy foot. I was glad I'd been out of the way up in the tree house when Pa and Grandpa and Mama'd talked it over. Mama was quiet now and sad, but somehow different. I thought maybe she was more determined looking.

Pa went off whistling, happy as a clam, to call Philip Atterbury home out of somebody else's backyard, the way he did nearly every night. Grandpa Thompson was rocking back and forth on the front porch faster than usual, and the rocker was scooting forward. Even if Mama hadn't said one word, I'd have known it was settled. We were going to Mojaveville. Pa was happy. Grandpa was worried.

"Where is Mojaveville?" I asked Mama.

"Who knows? Ask your father. He seems to know just about everything."

That settled that. I didn't say a word until the next morning; then I asked her again when Orrie and Wash and I came down to breakfast.

"I don't know where Mojaveville is. I told you last night, Callie. Your father said he'd look it up on a map."

"How's Pa going to do that if it's a brand-new place?" I wanted to know, pushing away Philip Atterbury who was trying to get my last slice of bacon. I lost. He snagged it off my plate.

Mama didn't even sigh. She just put down Philip Atterbury's own food and said, "I don't know, Callie. I don't see how it could be on a map yet, but I suppose your father'll find this Burdoo place all right, the jumping-off place, Hiram called it."

*　*　*

Pa did, too. Burdoo was San Burdoo, or really San Bernardino. It was a town about forty years old, settled by the Mormons, in the south and west cor- ner of San Bernardino County, a great big county even for California. It was a long way south from Sacramento, but that didn't faze Pa. He knew how to get there once he'd learned what the name of the town truly was and where it was. Pa was really rarin' this time.

He sold the house; then while Mama wandered around it, looking for the last time at things we'd had to sell along with it, we three kids went up into the tree house and said good-by to it, too. We were traveling light. Pa said we'd get what we needed in San Burdoo. All we took along were his carpenter's tools and our duds.

We took a sidewheeler down the muddy old Sac- ramento River and out across the blue windy bay to San Francisco, the place where Mama had some married brothers. There were a lot of relations there, but we said good-by to them fast. We'd moved around so much we hardly knew them. Us cousins just stood around and stared at one another. Then we got aboard another boat, a sailing ship this time, and went to the southern part of the state where it was browner and hotter. We didn't stay long in Los Angeles—just long enough for Philip Atterbury to

wander off and make us round him up by yelling
and whistling after him.

A stagecoach traveled from Los Angeles to San
Bernardino three times a week, and one morning
before it was really even light, we all piled aboard
and dragged our dog inside, too. Pa'd never been to
the bottom of California yet, so he rode up on top
with the driver—to spy out the countryside, he said.
I think, though, it was really to get away from
Philip Atterbury, who was barking to get out. I
looked out the window while we jerked and jolted
along, trying to spy out the countryside, too, but
didn't keep at it long. San Burdoo was more than
sixty miles east—as far as I could figure—sixty miles
of tall yellow dill weed, some lower, darker green
shrubs, orchards and farms and quail, hiding out
and calling "Bob-white." Sometimes we watered the
horses at creeks and springs where there were
pretty, feathery cottonwoods, and we stayed overnight the one night at a funny little mud-brick hotel
in a halfway place called El Monte. The next morning we were off again almost before the quail were
out.

San Bernardino wasn't anywhere near as big as
Sacramento. Wash and Orrie and I went exploring
while Pa and Mama went to the stores with Grandpa.

The streets weren't paved with bricks, and there weren't many trees either. Most of the houses had false fronts to make them look bigger than they were. A couple of biggish ones were made out of bricks, but most of them were wood. There were elegant gaslights, though, lit up on its streets. They made our faces turn bluish when we looked up at them. San Burdoo had a jail, which all of us tried to look inside until we got chased away by somebody. Orrie counted the general stores. There were seventeen. Wash looked for saloons; looking for them was his specialty. There were only twelve of them, he told me, as he came hauling Philip Atterbury along at the end of a rope to keep him from running away, the thing that dog did best.

"This is a real clean town," I said to Mama, who was waiting in the street for us when we came back to the biggest mercantile store, the one that sold dried beans and salt pork and pickles and stuff like that.

"Yes," said Mama. "I don't much mind the appearance of San Bernardino, although it certainly isn't San Francisco or Sacramento by a long shot." She looked at the snow-covered mountains around the town and drew a deep breath. "It might even have a high school."

"What's Pa doing? Where's Grandpa?" broke in Wash.

"Your father's paying up the bill," Mama told us, "and Grandpa's asking more questions about the mines." Her face was sour. "We've learned a few interesting things already about this Mojaveville of your Uncle Hiram's."

"What, Mama?" asked Wash.

She shook her head. "I don't want to talk about it. I'm not sure if what we've been told is the truth or just joshing. Whatever, we'll all learn soon enough. We'll stay over tonight at Starke's and Pine's Hotel here. I talked your father into that at least." Mama crooked her finger at me to come to her, then said to the others. "You two take Philip Atterbury walking some more. His constitution needs it from all that time he spent standing on my lap, drooling and sticking his head out the stagecoach window." Glad to get away, Orrie and Wash hurried down the street with our spotted dog leading them. He was big and long-legged, so it was easy for him to get ahead of Wash.

"Callie," Mama told me, "if Mojaveville is as bad as I'm beginning to suspect it is, I'm going to do something drastic."

I knew what *drastic* meant. Mama used the word

quite a bit. "What do you mean, Mama?" I was worried. When she said *drastic,* it usually meant just that.

"Well, we won't discuss it right now, Callie. Just you be prepared for drastic action. You know how I want you to get to high school someday."

"Yes'm," I told her.

Then she went back inside the store and left me outside with my nose stuck against the window, which had advertisements in it for Tutt's Pills for a Torpid Liver and Dr. Wood's Liver Regulator. I guessed folks in San Burdoo had bad livers all right, and maybe other bad insides, for down in one corner were great big bottles of Hostetter's Stomach Bitters and Simmons Nabob Pure Whiskey, the Family Medicine. I saw Mama inside frowning and pointing at both of those big bottles with a man clerk beside her writing down her order. This made me shiver. Things could get mighty drastic if Mama brought along Nabob Pure Whiskey. Mama didn't approve of whiskey even if it was for "medicinal purposes." Pa and Grandpa were bottle hiders. I think Grandpa Thompson would have tried to use our tree house except that his rheumatism kept him from getting up the ladder. We wouldn't have told on him.

Starke's and Pine's Hotel was a place that allowed Philip Atterbury inside, even when he stuck his head through the curtains in Wash and Grandpa's second-story room and howled at the moon half the night after the gaslights were turned off. In the morning Grandpa said that Philip Atterbury must have been affected by the moon. "Makes the danged mutt restlesser than ever," he complained to us at breakfast. "I didn't get much sleep last night 'cause of him." Grandpa twitched his shoulder. "That old wound 'a mine from Shiloh pains me today. Shouldn't 'a gone to war again. I was the oldest man in the Civil War—outside of some 'a the generals."

"He howled because he didn't like being shut up in that old stagecoach," Wash told Grandpa.

"We'll all like the mud wagon better, Wash," remarked Pa, attacking his eggs with his spoon, the way he usually did.

"Mud wagon!" exclaimed Orrie.

"A buckboard. Mud wagon's what they call it hereabouts. I rented us one." Pa spoke to Mama and Orrie and me. "There ain't much shade to a mud wagon. It'll be warm today. You females better keep out your sunbonnets."

Mama shot a hard look at Pa. "Hotter 'n Sacramento out here, Gideon?"

"Dry heat, Hope," he told her. "Mojaveville's out in the desert—high up, too. Dry heat ain't half so bad as the wet heat Sacramento has."

"We'll see," was Mama's only comment.

What Pa didn't tell us was that he'd hired a driver for the mule-pulled buckboard, too. He was a fat man with reddish blond whiskers and blue eyes that looked like they'd been out in the sunshine too much and had faded. His coat and pants were the dirtiest and dustiest I ever saw. So were his whiskers where they weren't stained brown with tobacco juice. He shook hands with Grandpa and nodded his head to Mama and me when he drove up to our hotel, then he said, "Eli Neuberger's my name, but folks in Mojaveville call me Slum Gullion Slim. I make the best slum gullion stew in the Mojave. I use anythin' that comes to hand. Gopher meat—that's just about the best, though."

"Oh," was all Mama said, and she didn't say it strongly.

Pa lifted me and Orrie and Wash into the back of the buckboard, which didn't have any shade over it at all, and we settled down on sacks of lumpy potatoes and coffee beans and whatever else Pa'd bought and Ma'd told me privately cost three times what it did back home in Sacramento. Then Pa lifted Mama on the second seat and hoisted Grandpa up next to her. Grandpa held Philip Atterbury by his collar.

"Sure don't fancy dogs back there among the expensive groceries," he grumbled to us.

"Oh, Grandpa, he's housebroke," whined my brother, but it didn't do him any good. Philip Atterbury stayed next to Grandpa Thompson.

"Maybe he ain't wagon broke, Wash."

When Pa swung up, too, Slum Gullion Slim told him, "They's a lot of folks these days headin' for Mojaveville. Four other mud wagons left already this mornin'. But they ain't many famblies goin' in that way yet, and I sure ain't seen many dogs. What're you folks called?"

Pa told him and sort of introduced us while Slim loosened the reins on his two mules, and we headed north out of San Bernardino. Slim's eyebrows rose up when he heard what we kids were called, but he nodded when Pa told him we were named after states. "Makes good sense to me, Mr. Perkins," he said. "As good a way as any to keep track of 'em. Not bad names at all for young 'uns, but what about that there dog 'a yours—Atterboy, you called him. What's he named after?"

Orrie piped up before I could get my hand over her mouth. "His name's not Atterboy, it's Atterbury.

He was named after the first boy that ever kissed Callie. She gave our dog the name."

"I was only ten years old," I told Slim.

"But she never forgot it," Orrie said so loud half of San Bernardino could have heard her. "Nobody's kissed her since."

"You shut up," I whispered to her, then to change the subject I called out to Slim. "Do you know our uncle, Hiram Perkins?"

He laughed, throwing his head back so far his hat fell off into Mama's lap. "The Duke 'a Kansas? Sure I know him."

"Duke of Kansas!" Pa said. "Hiram?"

"Yep, that's what we call him in Mojaveville. He says he was born in Kansas." Slim looked Pa in the face now and asked, as if maybe he'd made a mistake, "He was, wasn't he?"

"Yeah, I guess Hiram was," agreed Pa finally. "He came along after I did. Our folks had moved out of Texas by the time Hiram showed up in this world."

"Well, if there's any one thing I can say for you Perkinses, you sure move around, don't you?" Slim commented, sounding as if he approved.

"We sure do, Mr. Neuberger. We sure do. I wonder what they'll call you in Mojaveville, Gideon," said Mama, poking Pa with her parasol. She put it up a minute later and turned around to tell Orrie and me to get on our sunbonnets.

It was getting hot already, though it was only eight o'clock in the morning.

We started to climb once we left San Bernardino behind us. Finally with our behinds getting mighty sore from the jouncing of the mud wagon, which didn't have any springs, we got up to what Slum Gullion Slim called Cajon Pass. There was some tall timber there all right, and Wash asked him if Mojave-ville was nearby.

"No siree, sonny. We've got us some desert to cross yet after we get out 'a the pass. We'll camp here at the top of the pass and get an early start in the morning."

I liked the cool air of the pass. Mama had to tell Orrie and me to put on our shawls, and it was cold in our blankets that night, making my teeth chatter as I tried to keep warm under the mud wagon.

Down, down went the mules and buckboard the next morning. Philip Atterbury barked to get loose, and Grandpa finally tied him to the seat so he could stop holding him while he rared around. Down all the way to the Mojave River we kept going. It was getting warmer all the time now that we were way out of the hills. The ground was mostly flat and grayish, but there were bright-colored rocks around. Plants I never had seen before were leaning every which way. Some of them were really funny look-ing, tall and skinny. Others were just plain tall with arms sticking out all over them. Slim told me that the first skinny kind was Spanish bayonet. The Mojave Indians made soap out of it and ate its fruit and flowers. The kind that grew in groves, the one with arms, was a Joshua tree. The slender light green trees were mesquite, while the whitish bushes were saltbrush and pearlweed. The commonest plants of all were gray-green—sage and creosote bushes. High yellow yucca, almost as tall as Pa was, grew here and there, like fat candles.

"What kind 'a animals has this here desert got?" asked Wash.

Slim pointed up in the sky. "Look'a there, sonny. That black speck's a raven, I bet you, or maybe a hawk. There's other things too here—foxes and chuckawalla lizards, horned toads and pack rats— lots of rattlers and some gila monsters."

"Great heavens," I heard Mama mutter. "At least they won't be pets, I imagine."

"What about the Indians?" asked my sister. "Will we see them where we're going, Mr. Slim?"

"Sometimes," replied our driver. "They do a little farming—punkins and beans and things like that. They come up to Mojaveville to sell us stuff some-times."

"Are they dangerous?" asked Mama.

"Not much no more, mam. They got tamed fast enough. There's a U.S. Army fort not too far away."

"Well, I suppose we can take some comfort in that, Mr. Neuberger." Mama seemed a little more satisfied, but still she had a frown on her face while she fanned herself with her hand.

The desert was sure hot, even in April. So hot Pa was mopping at his face, while sweat ran down into Grandpa's beard. I was melting in my calico dress. Philip Atterbury's tongue hung out. Pa'd been right. The heat *was* dry, but it was still mighty hot.

"Guess you're sort of warm, huh, folks?" Slim asked us. "Well, jest you hang on a while longer. We'll be at Bass Ponds soon and we'll camp there. It ain't dried up yet. This here Mojave Desert ain't all pure desert. There's some water here and there, and at Bass Ponds there's fish and trees. It'll be your last chance to see swimmin' fishes."

Before Mama asked him, I did. " 'Last chance,' what does that mean?" The way Mama was thinking was catching.

He laughed again, a funny sort of laugh. "Last

chance to eat fish, little gal. There sure ain't no fish in Mojaveville, less'n it comes in a barrel—pickled."

Bass Ponds was as nice as he said. We camped there under the cool cottonwoods and mesquite trees, and we kids got our feet in the water. Then we set out again for Mojaveville in the morning.

"I guess there aren't any lakes near Mojaveville," I said to Orrie.

"Guess not, Callie."

"Not even a river, huh?" I liked rivers and ponds.

We kept on traveling north toward some moun-tains. The sky was such a bright blue it made my eyes hurt to look up at it. After a while I could make out colors in the mountains. They were funny look-ing all streaked like a mixed-up rainbow—orange, green, blue, yellow, rust color, cream color, red and brown and violet.

"Is that where Mojaveville is?" I called out to Slim.

"That's where it is, all right, up by them fancy mountains. Ain't they somethin', though?"

"Those are the strangest-looking hills I ever saw," commented Grandpa, shaking his head.

"Ah, you get used to 'em. After a while you even find yourself likin' 'em," Slim told him. "They look diff'rent at sunset and at diff'rent times of the day."

"They're horrible," said Mama, mostly to herself.
"They look like a crazy quilt a lunatic made."

Now we started to climb a little again. Finally
Slim hauled in the reins at the entrance to a narrow
canyon of rose-colored crumbly rock. "Here you
be," he announced. "This is where Mojaveville is."

"Where?" asked Pa, glancing around the way all
the rest of us were doing. There wasn't any town
that we could see.

Slim waved toward the top of the canyon. "Up
there. That's where the silver is."

"Up there!" exclaimed Mama.

"Sure, mam. Mojaveville's on a ledge. It's a purty
steep climb up the road for my mules and your supplies. I'd appreciate it if you folks'd get out and
walk the rest of the way."

We were too astonished to say anything, so we all
got down and began to climb up the narrow twist-
ing red road. We climbed up and up, the dirt slipping under our shoes, and then all at once, as
Grandpa put it later, "the glory of Mojaveville
shone about us!"

Not one of us said a word. There wasn't anything
we could do but gasp at the sight. Mojaveville was a
terrible eyeful. There wasn't one tree to be seen and
not one blade of grass on that pink ledge, nothing

but a few dirty gray-green looking bushes growing down the sides of a fifteen-foot drop. There were tents everywhere on the ledge, though, on the two sides of what was supposed to be a street. A couple dozen houses had been built, rickety and half-nailed together. Two of them looked to me to be hanging over the edge of the canyon. But the strangest thing of all I saw were the big black holes in the side and back walls of the canyon around the ledge. Pink dust filled our noses. Pink pebbles hurt our feet. Our calico skirts and Pa's and Grandpa's coat tails blew in the hot wind.

When Slum Gullion Slim finally drove his team past us and yelled out, Mojaveville woke up a little. Men came out of the tents to stare, and to my surprise half a dozen of them came crawling out from behind boards, which half blocked up the caves.

"Great heavens, those holes aren't mine entrances at all," I heard Mama gasp out. "They're really caves. Folks are living in them!"

"Sure, mam," Slim told her, "Caves is cooler'n houses—lots cooler. You folks just stay right here and I'll round up the Duke. It won't take long. That there's the Lion's Den up ahead—the cave with the barrel staves propped up in front of it."

"That's a hotel?" asked Wash.

"Sure, one of the best in Mojaveville," explained
Slim. "But it ain't a lodgin' house for ladies and
young 'uns, jest for gents. The Duke'll have somethin' fixed up for ya—even if it is Sunday. The Duke
gits things done."

He got down and left the mules, who drooped
their heads looking at Mojaveville just the way we
drooped ours. Even Philip Atterbury was sagging as
if he didn't like what he saw either.

While I waited for Uncle Hiram to come, I turned
around and looked behind me to get some relief.
Way off in the distance, miles away, I knew lay San
Bernardino beneath the blue mountains, but below
me there was nothing but a dry lake, covered white
with alkali. Beyond it there was a greenish line that
was the Mojave River's trees. The view in that direction wasn't much, but the view in front of me
was lots worse.

Uncle Hiram showed up right away with Slim.
He hadn't changed much except that he was dirtier,
dirtier than even Slum Gullion Slim, though he
wore a top hat and a frock coat with a velvet collar.
He had a scraggly brown beard and the Perkins'
pointy nose and needed a haircut worse'n usual.
Other than that he looked the same. He shook hands
with Pa and Grandpa Thompson, then hugged Orrie

and Wash and me. He smelled of whiskey and dust. Then he started to grab Mama to kiss her, but she stepped back so he couldn't.

"No, you don't, Hiram Perkins!" she told him. "This is the Creator's dumping ground! You tricked us all. This is the worst place you found yet. I'd rather be kissed by a hog than by you." Her eyes blazed sparks at him. "Where's this tall timber you wrote us about—you, you Duke of Nowhere."

"Ah, Sis," Hiram said, "that was only somethin' I put in the letter I sent you folks to fancy it up. I ain't much of a letter writer. You know that. There ain't no timber here. It all gets wagoned in from Burdoo." He turned to Pa. "Gid, they'll be plenty 'a work fer ye. We got lumber here. Can start to work tomorrow, if ya like, doin' whatever kind 'a carpentering you want."

"Gideon," Mama spoke through her teeth. "Gideon, I want to go back to San Bernardino at once."

"Ah, come on, Sis, don't be that way. You're spoilin' everybody's fun. There's real opportunities up here," came from the Duke.

"You keep your long nose out of this, Hiram," Mama said, not taking her snapping eyes from Pa's face. "Gideon, I'm talking to *you*. We're going back right now."

"You givin' me orders now, Hope?" Pa asked her.

"I'm doing just that!"

Pa shifted his position so he stood a little bit closer to Hiram. "I ain't takin' orders from you. I'm the man of this house. I earn the living so I'm the one to give orders."

Mama's face had been as red from the heat as everybody else's. It got white now. "In that case, the children and I will go back—alone. I promised you, Gideon, before we left San Bernardino that I would do something drastic if this camp was what the store clerks hinted it might be."

"What'll you use for money?" he asked her. "You know it took most of what we had to get here. I only got about twenty dollars left. You got any cash on you, Hiram?" Pa looked at the Duke of Kansas.

Before Hiram could answer, Mama started talking "I wouldn't take one red cent from Hiram Perkins or whatever he calls himself up here in this hideous place." She stared around herself again and shuddered. "This Creator's dumping ground!" Mama held out her hand to Pa. "Give me ten dollars, Gideon."

Although Pa was as strong willed as she was, he reached down into his pocket and gave her a ten-dollar gold piece, then turned his back on her to look at the San Bernardino Mountains as if he was seeing them for the first time.

"It's too late to start back today," Mama said to Slim, who'd stood by listening to every word of the fight. "Where's another hotel? My husband is stay-ing with his brother, the Duke, in the Lion's Den."

"There really ain't one yet for ladies," he replied, "but Miss Jennieveva can put you up maybe. She's got that new house up yonder, the big one with the finished front porch."

Mama nodded. "I'm much obliged to you, Mr. Neuberger. I think I'll go back with you tomorrow with half of our supplies." She grabbed Philip At-terbury's rope from Grandpa, nodded again for Wash, Orrie, and me to follow her. We came along at her skirts, but Grandpa didn't. He started to, then stopped, and looked down at his dusty boots.

"Are you coming with us, Father?" she called back to him.

Grandpa looked up now. His face wasn't the least bit happy. "No, Hope. I guess I'm stayin' with Gid and Hiram. I don't approve of what you're doin', leavin' your husband."

Mama's eyes got slit-narrow she was so mad. "My *own father! Men!*" she thundered. She whirled around and grabbed Wash by one ear and gave a fast tug at Philip Atterbury's rope that made him flop over then tag along at her heels. Fast as we could walk, we headed for the big house with the porch.

2 * Miss Jennieveva

Miss Jennieveva Acheson was the homeliest lady I
ever had seen in all my life. She had mouse-brown
hair, but not enough of it. What there was she had
piled up on top of her head in a skinny braid. She
braided it as loosely as she could and to make it look
bulkier put in some false hair that wasn't quite the
right color, but it still didn't do any good. Her face
was long and horsey, and her neck real long, too. Her
eyes were little and squinty and greenish, I guess,

and her mouth was sort of like a mousetrap, though why I thought it was I couldn't ever explain to Orrie.

Miss Acheson finally turned out to be our best friend in Mojaveville. We found out that she always wore black taffeta dresses and lace collars, sort of funeral dresses, just like the one she wore on that terrible Sunday when Mama and the rest of us, including Philip Atterbury, were brought into her parlor by her Chinese servant, who bowed to us, hissed, and went away right off. To add to everything else that made Miss Jennieveva seem strung-out, she was wearing a pair of dangling jet earrings, which hung nearly to her shoulders. Later I found out she owned only two pairs of earrings, both long dangling ones, black onyx and jet.

"Who'd you be?" she asked Mama politely enough before Mama had got her temper back enough to talk.

"Hope Thompson," Mama told her, her eyes still snapping.

I gasped. Mama hadn't been that mad for a long, long time. She must really have been sore at Pa to take back her maiden name.

"Are these here your kids?" asked Miss Acheson, staring at us.

Mama nodded toward each of us in turn. "Yes, they're Callie, Orrie, and Wash Perkins."

"Perkins?" Miss Jennieveva's eyebrows raised up a whole inch.

"I have left my husband, Mr. Gideon Perkins," said Mama definitely.

"And you came up here to the mines *alone,* you and your children—and that animal, too?" Here she pointed at Philip Atterbury, who had his hind foot to his ear after a flea.

"No, we didn't. We left Mr. Perkins about five hundred feet down the street. We are sick and tired, sick and tired, I tell you, of moving around this entire country."

"Is your husband any kin to Hiram Perkins?" Miss Jennieveva made a worse face when she said our uncle's name than when she'd spoken about our dog.

"He certainly is!" Mama's eyes filled with tears.

Miss Acheson changed her ways in a minute after hearing this news. She came up to Mama, her skirts rustling, and put her arm around Mama's shoulders. We all sniffed the good smell about her then, even Philip Atterbury, who wrinkled up his nose trying to identify it. "You poor, poor dear," she said, comforting Mama. "You just go ahead and cry all you want to. My own father was a miner, a mover around, too. My mother used to say she never got to see a rosebush bloom properly. They never stayed long enough in one place. If your husband's any kin to Hiram Perkins, it's a wonder to me that you stayed with him as long as you did." Miss Acheson snorted. "The Duke of Kansas, indeed!"

I just had to know about our uncle and that new name he had in Mojaveville. "Mam, why's Uncle Hiram called a duke?"

"Because when he thought he'd struck it rich a week or two back, he went hog wild, spending money like he thought he was some lord from England. When his claim ran out, so did his credit. The name stuck, though."

"Oh." I was satisfied now. I'd guessed the money'd run out on Uncle Hiram from the dirt on him. When I'd seen him in his top hat and frock coat, I'd known he'd had some money one time from somewhere. But it was gone now. Besides if he was still rich, why was he living where he was living?

Orrie was just as curious as I was. "He got us down here from Sacramento," she told Miss Jennieveva. "What's the Duke doing now?"

Miss Jennieveva shrugged. "Working part time at one of the big mines around here, the Ace of Hearts or Silver Queen, when he isn't prospecting for an-

other strike out in the mountains around this ac-
cursed place."

Mama looked hopefully over her handkerchief at
Miss Acheson. "You don't like Mojaveville either?"

"Good gracious, no! This is a dreadful spot."

"Well then, if I may ask, why did you come here?
Did some man fool you into coming, too?"

Miss Jennieveva laughed. "I ran a boarding
house in Bodie until the silver ran out there." She
quit patting Mama and patted her braid instead.
"Let me tell you, I did very well there, very well
indeed, financially, that is. I came here to do the
same thing. When I've made the amount I want, I'll
sell out and go to San Francisco." She thought for a
moment, then added, "Or Seattle or Portland. I hear
tell there's more of an opportunity up there than in
the East nowadays."

"Opportunity for what?" Wash was real interested in Miss Jennieveva. I could tell by the way he
studied her. He hadn't ever seen anyone like her
before either. She was certainly something.

"None of your business, young man." Now she
turned to Mama. "I take it you all want rooms? For
how long, please?"

"Only overnight. We'll go back to San Bernardino
in the morning with Mr. Neuberger."

"You brought supplies and bedsteads and some

other things like that up here with you, didn't you, missus?"

"Yes. Gideon's going to share them with us. He'll take care of that." Mama frowned. "I suspect I can trust him that much."

"Come this way, please."

To our surprise Miss Acheson led us out of her front door again and up some steps at the side of the house. She opened another door and took us into a big room with one large bed, a washstand and basin, and two smaller beds, one set way up on top of the other. She looked down at old Philip Atterbury again and made another face. "Because it's only one night, he can stay here, too. Does he bark or howl?"

Wash figured it was only one night, so he lied. "No."

"What'll you do back in San Bernardino?" asked Miss Jennieveva of Mama. I noticed how careful she was not to call Mama either Miss Thompson or Mrs. Perkins. Miss Acheson sure had tact or maybe she was afraid of Mama's temper.

"There was a sign in one of the shops there that said they wanted a seamstress's helper."

"Well, Burdoo's not a bad town. I take it your husband'll stay here with his brother? Where's your husband stayin' at?"

"The Lion's Den."

"Might have guessed it. It's full of no-good men-folks."

"Pa's not no-good," flared Wash.

"And neither's Grandpa," came from Orrie.

"A grandfather, too?" Miss Jennieveva looked shocked for a minute, then nodded. "Well, my dears, I always did say the old ones were the worst ones. Another Perkins, I presume."

Mama sat down on the bed, still holding on to our dog. She didn't seem about to answer so I did. "No, mam, he's a Thompson, Mama's pa."

"The cruelest cut of all then—one's own flesh and blood!" said Miss Jennieveva with another nod. "The Lion's Den is the perfect place for your men-folks." She went to peer at herself in the mirror of our stuffy room and pick at her braid with her fin-gers. "The proprietor of that ghastly cave"—she shivered at her reflection and I could sure see why—"serves beans and whiskey for breakfast. He has no sheets on his bunks. Rattlesnakes even crawl in and sleep under the pillows in that place."

What she said got Mama up off the bed. "Gideon and Papa—they're in danger, then?" She sounded scared.

"Well, perhaps they are. Just the same I wouldn't worry my head too much about them."

"Well, I do!" Mama sat down again and let Philip

Atterbury go. He headed right for the open window and began to bark. After a while Mama went on, sniffling, "Whiskey and beans! Gideon's digestion! Oh my! Papa'll get sick, too. I just know he will!"

"Think you could get your husband and your father to move in here for the night? I had two mine owners go out this morning to San Francisco to see about getting some capital for a stamp mill. I run a good clean place, no cussing, no fighting, no drinking, and clean sheets every month. With water being hauled in here, selling for three cents a gallon, that's pretty good, even if I do say so. How about getting your menfolks in here if that's the way you feel."

Mama shook her head. She had a grip on herself now. "That isn't the way I feel. No, I won't go near either one of them." She took off her sunbonnet and put her hand over her eyes. Then she lost her grip on herself again and burst out, "I just can't leave Papa and Gid. You don't know them the way I do. They're helpless here, absolutely helpless. It could be the death of them both!"

"Helpless, my left hind foot!" Miss Jennieveva snorted so loud Mama looked up at her. "That's just what they want you to think. They want you to come running. They want you to wait on 'em and look after 'em. That's what men want all right."

"But I just can't leave them here to get sick or die! I can't run out on them, can I? It's my married duty to stay." Mama let out a deep sigh. "Whatever am I going to do?"

Miss Acheson's voice was as dry as Mojaveville's dust. "Seems you already made up your mind to keep an eye on 'em up here, don't it, my dear? Well, if you're going to be fool enough to stay on because of that, there's plenty of work here for ladies. That's probably what you'll have to do, go to work, isn't it? The mercantile store here, Ephraim Miller's place, needs a clerk, and I need some help, too." She looked Orrie and Wash and me up and down with her beady eyes. It was like being measured by a ruler inch by inch. "These here young 'uns 'a yours are big enough to do some work, too. I take it, missus, that your husband will help you some with expenses. If he won't, I know a judge in Burdoo who'll make him do it."

Mama said nothing to this advice. Wash did. "I don't want to work."

"Naturally you don't. It's in your nature not to want to work," Miss Jennieveva said. "After all, you are a lazy male, aren't you?" She seemed to think she'd spent enough time with us. "Well, folks, I got a boarding house to run and supper's coming up soon. You folks wash up, and come on down to eat."

"Oh, Miss Jennieveva, just a moment!" Mama had come alive a little more at the mention of food as we all had. "If we do stay here in Mojaveville, where'll we live? Do you have any ideas?"

Miss Jennieveva thought for a minute, then began to giggle, which sounded odd coming from her. "I do at that. I just remembered something I thought was queer at the time I heard it. The Duke of Kansas, he bought a house a while ago from a miner who sold out and went back East. I couldn't figure what he'd want with a house. It must 'a been for you folks. It isn't much of a house, though."

"I doubt if we could expect anything grand up here," said Mama. "At least it isn't a cave or a tent."

"You're darned tootin' there, missus. You can't expect much in Mojaveville. It could be worse than a cave, you know. Some menfolks have holed up in worked-out mines already. Quite a few of the mines around here didn't have too much silver in 'em."

"Miss Jennieveva, maybe Pa could add on to the house Uncle Hiram got for us? He's a carpenter, Pa is," I put in, because Mama's face was crumpling up again.

Miss Jennieveva giggled again. "Not this house— less'n he makes a pal out 'a Eva, and there's only one way to do that and that's to hang around her place."

"Who's Eva?" asked Mama.

"Our biggest saloon keeper, that's who."

"What's she got to do with our house?" I wanted to know.

"Your house's made out of the commonest thing Mojaveville's got."

"What's that?" I asked.

"Bottles, whiskey bottles!" Miss Acheson went out the door, then opened it again and stuck her long horsey head back inside. "I think I better introduce you to my boarders, missus, as Mrs. Perkins, who ain't a widow woman—yet. There's fifty men to every single lady in Mojaveville. Some of 'em are gettin' pretty tired of being bachelors. Single bless-edness is wearin'." She sighed, then she gave orders. "Boy," she was glaring at Wash. "You feed that mutt 'a yours out behind my kitchen after supper, do you hear?"

"Hey, Miss Jennieveva, ain't there any more kids up here?" Wash called out to her, ignoring her glaring at him, before she could shut her door on us again.

"Well, you ain't *quite* it, sonny! There's the Step-neys and there's Banjo."

We met Banjo after dinner when we all took

Philip Atterbury out behind the kitchen to feed him
his dinner of leftover deer *ragout,* or at least that's
what Miss Jennieveva called it, though it seemed
more to me like stew. Un Lung, who'd opened the
door to us in the first place, was a thin little China-
man who wore a dull blue blouse and a black fedora
hat. Banjo wasn't Chinese. He was dressed in a plaid
shirt and black derby. Where Un Lung had black
hair, yellow skin, and narrow black eyes, Banjo had
black hair, brown skin, and the biggest, roundest
brown eyes I ever saw. He looked at us when we
came through the kitchen door and bowed just the
way Un Lung did. I'd seen Indians before so I knew
Banjo was one, even if some of his manners were
sort of Chinese.

"You speak English?" Orrie stupidly asked him.

"Both 'a us do, me 'n Un Lung," said Banjo, reach-
ing for a dish towel and grabbing a plate Un Lung
handed him. "Miss Jennieveva taught Un Lung. I
got taught at school in Burdoo." He grinned when
he pointed at his chest. "I'm a Mojave! I'm a Indian."

"Have you scalped any folks?" Wash was fasci-
nated.

"Not me—my pa maybe before he died. I'm a
orphan." Banjo sure had white teeth when he
smiled. "Your pa shot anybody?"

"Nope. I don't think he shot anybody yet," confessed Wash, who found Banjo and Un Lung a lot more interesting than the men with whiskers and big mustaches who were Miss Acheson's boarders. All they talked about at the supper table was the price of silver and when Mojaveville would get a railroad.

"Then your pa ain't like Wyatt Earp?" Banjo seemed disappointed.

"He sure ain't. Our pa's only a carpenter," said Wash. "Do you know Wyatt Earp?" Wash's mouth hung open like a hooked fish's.

"Sure do. He comes up here to Mojaveville lots 'a times," Banjo told us. "He likes me."

"Wyatt Earp ever shot anybody up here?" asked Orrie.

"Not yet."

"You girls go feed Philip Atterbury," Wash ordered Orrie and me. "I got other things to do."

We went, knowing that he wanted to talk about gory details with Banjo Acheson. We knew Wyatt Earp was one of Wash's idols. He liked him even better'n Buffalo Bill in the dime novels because to his way of thinking Mr. Earp was "realer." Wyatt Earp didn't show up in circuses and sideshows and that kind of thing. The more a person showed himself in public, the "unrealer" he got to be. Wash had explained it once to me. Mr. Earp wasn't a showoff.

While Philip Atterbury stuffed himself, Orrie and I talked. It wasn't about Wyatt Earp either. We were both plenty worried about Mama's leaving Pa.

"What's gonna' happen, Callie?" she asked me, as we looked out at the mountains behind us, gone purple in the twilight so we couldn't make out the crazy-quilt colors anymore.

"I don't know," telling her the truth. Then I threw in for good measure, "I don't think Mama'll go back to Pa though—not so long as he's staying up here in Mojaveville."

"She's too mad at him." Orrie agreed with me.

"She sure is. He's gonna' have to give in to her."

"And he won't ever do that."

Orrie and I were shivering by now. We'd left our shawls upstairs in the room. One thing you could say about the Mojave Desert was that it had trouble deciding whether to roast you or freeze you.

Suddenly we both heard our first coyote howling somewhere down below us. "It ain't so friendly here as Sacramento," Orrie told me mournfully. "I wonder who the Stepneys are?"

"Folks who hole up in a cave, maybe?" I wondered about them, too, and was about to go on talking about them when all at once Wash came bursting out of the back door.

"Banjo! He just told me," he called out. "There ain't no school up here in Mojaveville—not even a schoolhouse." Wash was pleased as punch.

I wasn't. I only had a little while to go in grammar school, and I did want to go to high school—the way Mama wanted me to.

Orrie sort of liked school, too. "There ain't no reason for you to get so happy about that, Wash," she told him, taking the wind right out of his sails. "If we stay here, Mama'll start one."

"Yeah, Wash, she's done it before and she'll do it again," I put in.

"There's a big diff'rence this time, though, Callie. The other times she had Pa on the school board to help her out. Ladies don't get put on 'em, only men. This time she's gotta do it alone, and I bet she won't ask no favors of Pa or Grandpa or the Duke. Banjo says there ain't one teacher up here. Miss Jennieveva, she adopted him and she teaches him—when she can catch him." Wash laughed. "Mama's got a big job cut out for her this time."

"Well, Miss Jennieveva'll help Mama," I said. "Miss Jennieveva's worth any two men hereabouts." Wash didn't believe me. I could tell it by what I could see of his face in the dusk. "Maybe she's worth two even of old Mr. Wyatt Earp. She hates men!"

"Is that so!" he yelled at me. "Banjo told me something about her, too. You know what she's going after in San Francisco or Portland?"

Orrie stuck her tongue out at him. "What's she after?"

"A husband, that's what! She aims to buy herself one where there's the most men. It's the only way she can get one, is to buy one. With fifty men up here to every lady old Jennieveva's got to go away and buy one!"

I got awful mad when I heard this. It made me feel sorry for Miss Jennieveva, who couldn't help being homely. I spoke to Orrie, who'd understand. "Banjo's sure not a gentleman, is he?"

"Of course not, he's a Mojave Indian," Wash put in, before Orrie could agree with me. "Why should Banjo look out for that old lady? She works him, don't she, in the kitchen?"

"You're going to have to work, too, Washington," I cautioned him.

"Not too hard, I ain't. If Ma or that old lady work me too hard, I'm gonna take Philip Atterbury and move into the Lion's Den with Pa and Grandpa and the Duke. You can tell Ma I said it, too. Me and Philip Atterbury and the rest of us men got to stick together."

I counted up. That made five men, counting our dog, and only three of us weak females. "That isn't fair, Wash. There's only three of us."

"Yeah, but you got Miss Jennieveva. She's worth any two men and that makes five of you, too."

I had the last word, though, sweet as I could say it. "I'm sure glad you agree with me about Miss Acheson."

I had a little while to talk with Mama after we both crawled into the big bed. "What're we going to do now, Mama?"

"We're going to stay here and make the best of it and hope it won't be too long before your father sees the error of his ways." Her voice was sad.

"How long do you think that'll be?"

"I don't know, Callie, honey. Gideon's mule stubborn. He's at a new place and you know how he cottons to that. Even if he was alone up here, it'd take some time for him to get Mojaveville out of his system." Mama rolled over now and punched her pillow with her fist. "We could wait Gideon out on that, but it isn't so simple. There's Hiram, too, aiding and abetting your father. Now that he's got a good hold on him again, Hiram won't let him go— not by a long sight. It's always been this way with your father and Hiram and me—since before you were born."

"What's Uncle Hiram want with Pa?" I couldn't understand this talk at all.

"Hiram thinks the Lord's finest creation is an old bachelor. He never wanted your father to get married." Mama snorted. "He and Gideon had some great big plans. They were going to conquer the whole world together. Why do you suppose it's so easy for Hiram to act like a duke? Sometimes I think he believes he *is* one."

I had what I thought was a good idea so I sprung it on Mama. "Maybe if we could get Uncle Hiram married off to some lady?" I got up on my elbow. My brain was working fast. "What about Miss Jennieveva, Mama? Banjo told Wash she was looking hard for a husband."

"*Callie!*" Mama was really shocked at me. "Miss Acheson's a friend of ours!"

"But she does want a husband—real bad, too. Banjo says she's going to buy one, and Uncle Hiram spent all his money."

"I suspect Miss Acheson may want a husband at that, Callie, but remember she already knows Hiram. You couldn't spring him on her! Besides she's ten years older than Hiram, if she's a day. No,

even if they were the same age, I don't think Jennieveva would have a thing to do with the Duke of
Kansas."

Well, that took care of that. I changed the subject, but still didn't tell her what Wash had threat-
ened to do if he was worked too hard. She'd had a
bad enough day already. So I said to her, "How do
you s'pose we'll like living in a house made out of
old bottles?"

She sounded tired out. "I can't begin to guess,
dear. You know how I feel about folks drinking
liquor. If anybody'd ever told me I was to live in a
house that whiskey built, I'd never have believed it.
I just hope it won't be too warm in the summer for
us."

"Think Grandpa'll come back to live with us?"

"I do think that could happen any day now," she
answered me. "Beans never sat well on his stomach,
and he likes clean clothing and sheets sometimes,
too. Yes, Father'll be back, Callie."

"But what if we're all working? He'll get lonesome. What'll he do?"

"He'll have to go out prospecting. He's not too old
for that. This dry climate ought to be good for his
rheumatism. Anyhow I'm going to try to convince
him of that. Half of his aches and pains are in his

mind. I'll go see Mr. Miller at his store tomorrow,
but even if I get the clerk's job, I won't make much
money—not enough to support all of us. Grandpa'll
have to pull his weight, too, particularly after you
and Orrie and Wash start school this fall. We can't
expect your father to give us all of what he makes.
We're going to pay rent to Hiram, what's more. I
won't have his charity."

"But, Mama," I protested, "there isn't any school
up here—not even a schoolhouse. Didn't you know
that? Banjo told Wash."

Mama's voice sounded half-strangled she was getting so mad. "I knew that the minute I got my first
look at this awful place. There'll be a teacher and a
school somehow, though, even if there won't be a
schoolhouse. That can come later. I'll take it up
with Miss Acheson." She was quiet for a little bit,
then she said, "Callie, did you ever hear what Presi-
dent Garfield said about a school?"

"No, I never did."

"Well, he said if you put a child at one end of a
log and a teacher at the other, you've got a school."

"There aren't any trees up here, though."

Mama laughed in the dark. "Sometimes even if
you have Thompson looks I think you have Perkins
'no-imagination.' It was only his special way of say-

ing things. Perhaps you'll go to school in a cave or even in a mine, sitting on a rock. All the same you'll go to school."

"It takes a school board to get a teacher and start a school, and men are on school boards, aren't they? I don't think men care so much about schools, specially bachelors who haven't got any families." I'd heard about school boards in Sacramento.

"Men are on school boards." Mama grunted her answer. "But there won't always be only men running the world. Someday, Callie, women'll be able to vote and be on school boards, too. I don't know that I'll see that day, but I'm sure you and Orrie will."

I was very interested in the notion of my voting. I'd seen an election in Sacramento. It was fun. I liked brass bands marching down the street and American flags and the G.A.R. out in their blue Union uniforms, and red, white, and blue bunting. I even liked some of the orators from the G.A.R.

Sighing, Mama reached out in the dark and patted me on the shoulder. "Don't you worry about school. Somehow—I don't really know how yet— I'm going to see you and Orrie and Wash through high school. I'll take it up with Miss Jennieveva in the morning."

I wasn't really sleepy yet. I was too keyed up by
what had happened that day and could have talked
more with Mama. But I didn't get to do any talking
because right then, and all of a sudden, up came the
full moon over the mountains. It was as round and
as yellow as Mama's ten-dollar gold piece.

It set Philip Atterbury off, of course. He'd been
asleep on Miss Jennieveva's hooked rug. Now he
woke up.

Because our bed was on the way to the window,
he jumped up on it and tromped across our stom-
achs, let himself down wheezing, put his front paws
on the windowsill, and started to howl at the moon.

"I hope they hear him all the way to the Lion's
Den," I told Mama.

"Go to sleep—if you can, Callie."

I tried to, but wasn't able to make it for a long
time. I knew Mama was crying, for now and then
her side of the bed shook a little bit, but because of
our dog's noise I couldn't hear her. I wondered how
Pa and Grandpa were doing down in the Lion's
Den.

I wondered, too, if they missed us as much as I
missed them. In the dark I said my prayers and
blessed them just the same, even Uncle Hiram, just
as if there hadn't been any fight at all. Maybe that'd

3 ✳ Grandpa Thompson

We had breakfast at Miss Jennieveva's—flannel cakes and, because she kept her own hens, big brown eggs. Then we all had a little talk after her gentlemen boarders had gone off to the mines or wherever else they worked.

"See here, Missus Perkins," she told Mama, "I don't figure you've got a lot of money. What you owe me for last night's lodging and your meals you

keep the rattlers off them that night, but l
feeling it wouldn't be any help in their no
whiskey for breakfast.

don't have to pay me now. Your young 'uns can make it up when you all start earning wages from me."

Wash was concerned about this working. "What're we supposed to do?" he demanded. There was a sour look on his face when he spoke.

"You, young man, will run errands for me."

"What kind 'a errands, mam?"

"Oh, taking lists of things I need to Miller's store. You be here at eight o'clock in the morning for a couple of hours."

"Sundays too?"

"No Sundays."

"What d'ya pay?"

"Five cents an hour."

"Oh. That ain't very much." Wash was good at arithmetic when he wanted to be. "That's only 'bout fifty—sixty cents a week, ya know."

"I can add as well as you, my boy," Miss Jennie-veva told him.

He would have argued, but Mama stopped him. "That's a fair wage, Washington. Now, Miss Ache-son, what do you have in mind for my girls?"

"Un Lung has his hands full in the kitchen in the mornings. Banjo helps, of course, but he ought to have his lessons with me then. I thought your youngest one could help Un Lung. Seven cents an hour for that job, that's what I'll pay."

"Doing what?" asked Orrie, as glowering as Wash had been.

"Helping Banjo scour pots, but peeling spuds mostly. My paying guests sure do eat a heap of spuds."

"Yes, I noticed how they ate potatoes," agreed Mama. "And what of Callie?"

"Callie's a big strong girl." My heart sank on hearing her words. She went on without mercy. "Callie will be able to make beds and tidy up rooms better'n any Mojave Indian girl I could get." Miss Jennieveva's eyes got narrower now. She turned suddenly to me. "You know how to make up beds?"

"Yes'm," I told her. I'd rather make beds and clean her boarders' rooms than peel dirty old spuds. I thought Orrie'd got the worst bargain of all. So did she, judging by the look on her face.

"Well, even if you can't, my dear, I can soon teach you," Miss Jennieveva went on talking to me. "You seem to be a bright child. Because of that I'll pay you a whole ten cents an hour."

I wanted to say, "I am bright. I get all A's, mostly." But I didn't—not in front of Mama, who didn't like braggers.

"You young 'uns all start work day after tomorrow," announced Miss Acheson.

"But what shall I do?" Mama wanted to know.

"Some fancy ironing, my corset covers, petticoats,
shirtwaists. Twenty-five cents an hour for that fancy
work. The Chinese across the canyon here in Mojaveville do most of my laundry, but they don't iron
to suit me. I don't think people in China even know
what ruffles are." Miss Jennieveva poured Mama another cup of coffee.

"With water selling for three cents a gallon, how
can *anyone* do laundry?" asked Mama, blowing on
her coffee.

"I think by the looks I've had of most of the folks
in Mojaveville that they don't do any. Once a month
I send sheets and towels and table linens to Barstow
to have them washed." She laughed. "It's expensive,
but cheaper than doing them here. After all, my
Forty-Niner pa used to send his shirts from San
Francisco to Honolulu in the Sandwich Islands to
be washed. Barstow's not that far away. My boarders patronize Un Lung's relations." She shivered. "I
think they don't ever change the rinse water."

"Hey Mama, what about baths? Do folks have to
take 'em up here?" asked Wash, cramming a third
corn muffin into his mouth.

"Seldom, all too seldom," said Miss Jennieveva. "Some of the men hereabouts say dirt keeps you healthy. Some of the others say it gets too hot in the summer here to perspire, so you don't need baths."

Miss Jennieveva was sure outspoken. I gasped to hear her say *perspire* right out. It was almost as bad as saying *sweat*.

"Now that I come to think about it, there is one solution to the bath problem. Some folks use it," she went on.

"What's that?" asked Wash.

"Bass Ponds. Some men take a bar of soap and go there and jump in. That way they wash their duds, too."

Wash thought that idea sounded pretty good. In any case, he liked being dirty. Mama didn't. I could tell by the look on her face that she didn't much fancy the idea of Bass Ponds either. But I still couldn't see how we were going to be able to afford a Saturday night bath, not with what water cost in Mojaveville. Maybe it'd have to be Bass Ponds for us after all.

We got Philip Atterbury, who was a real sleepy dog, on the end of his rope and after breakfast started out to the house Uncle Hiram had got for us. It wasn't hard to find. It was the only bottle house

in the camp and was up a ways from Miss Jennieveva's, on a little ledge. It glittered in the sunshine,
full of rainbow colors.

"Good heavens, look at that!" Mama exploded.
"It's unbelievable."

It sure was. Whiskey bottles of every kind under
the sun poked their bottoms out along the side of
our house as we climbed up the slope to it. The door
wasn't made of bottles, of course. It was wood and it
was half open. Mama pushed it the rest of the way,
and in we went. After all it was our house, wasn't
it?

Inside it was even more amazing. The bottles had
been set close together in mortar. We never did
know the man who built our house, but as Mama
said, he sure had a strange eye for color. One whole
wall was made of yellow bottles. Standing where
the light came through it was like standing in a sunset. Another wall was all green bottles. I thought
that standing by it was like being under a waterfall.
The other two walls were bottles all mixed up
together—bluish and greenish and white and a sort
of pale lavender. The place had two rooms, a
kitchen and living room together and one little back
room that was a bedroom, I guessed. It was made of
mixed-up color bottles, too.

"Look's like somebody's gonna' have to make

friends with Eva whatever-her-name is," Orrie whispered to me. "We're gonna' need some more room."

"Uncle Hiram prob'ly introduced Pa and Grandpa
to her last night," was what I had to say.

Pa already had been to the bottle house with
Slum Gullion Slim and the mud wagon. There were
shelves in the kitchen. Somebody'd put beans and
coffee and things on them in bags, and canned stuff,
too, above the sheet-iron stove. Mama and Pa's bed-
stead was put together and a mattress was on top of
it. Our three little mattresses and some blankets
were on the floor. All of the pots and pans we'd
bought in San Bernardino were there, too, on top of
the stove.

Mama was furious. *"Gideon!"* she yelled out.
"Gideon's been here. He was *that* sure I wouldn't go
back to San Bernardino! He dumped all of our stuff
here."

"Oh, don't go blaming Pa," came from Wash. "It
ain't his fault. He thought he was doin' us a favor. I
remember now what I was supposed to tell you,
Mama. Banjo, he told me while I fed Philip Atterbury this morning after we ate breakfast. Miss Jennieveva—she sent Banjo down to the Lion's Den last
night to tell Pa we were stayin' in Mojaveville.
Then she sent him to Mr. Miller's store this morning

to say that there was a poor tricked-by-a-man lady in town that could take his clerkin' job. You got hired at twenty cents a hour."

Mama was almost as mad now as when she'd just walked away from Pa. "Well, that Miss Acheson does take a great deal on herself, doesn't she? Why didn't she tell me what she'd done?" But Mama put her hand to her cheek and laughed, looking around at our house. "Well, I suppose she meant to do me a good turn. The house that whiskey built! We certainly won't need any address or doorbell, will we? Anyone can tell we're at home just by looking in through a bottle."

"No, they can't, Mama," Orrie told her with her eye to a green bottle. "I can't look out, so nobody can look in."

Mama didn't say anything more about the house. Neither did I, but I'd noticed something very interesting about it already. It was cooler inside it, even with the door open, than it was outside. I sat down on one of the two rickety old chairs by the door under the green wall, the coolest-looking one.

"Makes you look like a pole bean, sittin' there," my nice brother said.

"Oh, go outside in the sun and shrivel up," I told him. "Mama,"—I looked around at the bottle walls and down at the dirt floor—"this house'll be easy to keep clean. Bottles don't catch a lot of dust—not bottles stuck on their sides in mortar."

"Thank heaven for small favors," said Mama. "Several small favors—not having to see Gideon Perkins today and the errands Miss Jennieveva had Banjo do for me." She looked at my brother as she untied the strings of her sunbonnet. "By the way, Wash, did Banjo happen to tell you when the 'poor tricked-by-a-man lady' was to come to work?"

"Tomorrow morning at eight o'clock," answered Wash.

Mama put her hands on her hips and looked about her. "Then it looks as if we're going to have time to do some fancy house cleaning, doesn't it?"

Wash let out a moan. There was nothing he liked less than housework. In that way he was like Pa and Grandpa. All men, according to Mama, seemed to think the Brownies came in the middle of the night and did the sweeping and dusting and scrubbing. Ladies knew better.

Mama took pity on Wash when I wouldn't have. She sent him off to Miss Acheson's for the bucket of water we'd need to drink and get supper with. Orrie and Mama and I did the work. He took so long coming back home that I guessed he'd made a detour by the Lion's Den.

Mama went to Eph Miller's the next morning all dressed up in her gray silk dress. She thought maybe it was a mite fancy for clerking in the store, and so did I. Maybe calico would've suited better, but then we both agreed it was important to make a good impression the first day on a job.

She seemed plenty worried when she put on her hat with the white rosebuds on it, her best one.

"What's the matter, Mama?" I asked her.

She looked mournful. "Callie, I never worked a day in my life before. Maybe I'll get dismissed right off."

I was shocked. "Oh, no, you won't, Mama. You're a good worker."

She shook her head. "I never was much good at arithmetic in school. Over the years I doubt if I've got any better."

I was even more shocked at this information. I thought because she'd wanted to be a teacher, she'd be a good arithmeticker. "But, Mama, you were going to be a teacher!"

"A high school teacher, Callie—that's what. A literature teacher. I was going to go on to normal school after I went through high school."

I gasped. We hadn't dreamed that Mama aimed to be college educated. No Perkins had ever gone to college—no Thompson either.

"Did Grandpa know this?" I had to find out.

"Yes, Callie, he knew it. So did my mother."

"What'd they think?"

"Your grandpa said it wasn't much use educating women. They only went out and got married before they did anything with what they learned." Mama jabbed a hatpin through her hat. We didn't have a mirror yet, but she did a good job of it and didn't stab herself in the head. "Your grandmother thought I was the sauciest thing in petticoats." She laughed. "All the same she seemed a little bit proud of me because I had such notions." Now Mama scowled. "But then I met Gid Perkins!"

"Pa'll be coming into Miller's store," I warned her.

"Let him! I'll look holes through him—your grandpa and that Duke of Kansas, too. And don't you go near them either! Now you children, get on over to Miss Jennieveva's. I'll do the best I can at Miller's, and you three do the very best you can at her place."

I guessed what she meant, and said, "We're prov-ing something to Pa, aren't we?"

"We sure are, Callie," she told me. "We're show-ing him and all the rest of the Lion's Den what we're made of." And she marched right out of our bottle house, her back straight as a rifle barrel, off to

Miller's Mercantile Store, leaving me to shake the beans out of the sack to soak for supper that night. The water wagon had showed up early, and we'd bought a whole big bucket.

"Sure hope Miss Jennieveva feeds us," Wash said.

"Don't worry. She will," I said to him, "or if she doesn't, we can make do. I can make sandwiches, remember?"

"Out of what?" asked Orrie. "There ain't any bread here yet."

"Well, there will be tomorrow," I told her. "I'll borrow a riser from Un Lung. We've got lots of flour."

I did, too. Un Lung gave me some riser after I'd spent my hours with Miss Jennieveva making beds, airing pillows, and bashing the pink dust out of her carpets on the line with a carpet beater. Un Lung was really nice to her, Orrie told me. He made jokes all the time and fed her cookies. He had Banjo instead of her scrub out the big roasting pans with sand while she got to scour the breakfast plates. That was the way Miss Jennieveva did dishes—sand first to get off the food and grease, then water rinsing at the last.

"And there's some real news," Orrie whispered to

me once, when I came out to hang up some bed-
spreads.

"What's that? Uncle Hiram move in here this
morning?"

"Oh, no, it's not anything like that. It's that Miss
Jennieveva's orderin' out a bathtub from San Burdoo. She sent Wash to Miller's with the order. Wash
told me."

"Oh, what's so great about that—a bathtub?" I
asked her.

"It'll be the only bathtub in Mojaveville!"

I nodded. I couldn't say anything, because I had
my mouth full of clothespins. That really was news
then, though I supposed I'd have to add cleaning it
out to my list of chores.

Our work wasn't too hard. Un Lung fed us sandwiches of corned beef. We missed not having any
milk, but he made us a drink out of canned milk and
water.

"No cow in Mojaveville," he told us. "No cow—
because no grass."

Banjo ate lunch with us, too. "When do the Mo-
javes bring green things up here to sell?" I asked
him.

"In summertime. The squaws bring 'em," he told
me.

Banjo Acheson could play the banjo, which is

how he got his nickname. The only piece he knew all the way through, though, was "Swanee River." I could tell by the way Edgar Acheson, which was his real name, snorted when he said the word *squaws* that he thought all girls were squaws. I didn't like that. I'd teach him better manners before I was through with him, so I asked him, "What grade'll you be in, Banjo, when school starts next fall?"

His jaw dropped almost to his belt. "What school?"

"The school Mama and Miss Jennieveva are going to start."

Hearing this news didn't set well with him. He jammed that derby of his down over one side of his head and yelled at me, sticking his face in mine. "There ain't gonna' be no school!"

"Yes, there is," I told him. "You just keep on hoping that there won't be, Banjo, and you'll be doomed to disappointment."

"Ah, go on home, Callie," he said, scowling at me.

So then we did get up and go. I wasn't afraid that Banjo might get me in bad with Miss Acheson. She and Mama would be on the same side when it came to schooling, I knew, and besides that morning she'd said I was a "good worker" twice.

Then she'd gone on to say, "It won't be long at all,

Callie, before you Perkins folks pay me back what you owe me. Then I'll start payin' you right out." She looked at me hard. "You know that what I'm doin' is the business way, don't you? You have to do things the business way. Now don't you kids go pesterin' your ma up at Miller's either. That wouldn't be a bit businesslike."

"Yes'm," I said. I didn't see why she had to go and say that. We Perkinses were honest people. I hadn't expected not to pay her back and for a minute I got a little bit mad, but it didn't last. I figured this was probably her funny way of being nice, sort of apologizing for not paying us and warning us, too.

First thing I did at home was let Philip Atterbury out, then straighten up the house. Wash and Orrie went outside with the dog and watched the mule-team ore wagons go by down to Daggett, where a stamp mill was. They thought it was exciting, watching the drivers pull back on the reins and haul on the wagon brake to keep the heavy wagons from shooting too fast down Mojaveville's steep grade. I wasn't as interested in ore wagons and mules, and I didn't like the language one of the swampers used as he came up to our house. Orrie had put her fingers in her ears, but I'd seen Wash say the words over and over quietly, only moving his lips.

Orrie came in from outside pretty soon. Her face was so pink I made her sit down because I was afraid of her getting sunstroke. "Callie, do you think we ought to go call on the Stepneys?" she asked.

"No, siree," I told her. "Whoever they are, they came to Mojaveville before we did. If they want to get to know us Perkinses, they'll have to look us up." I stopped sweeping the floor and thought a little bit. Then I said, "Leastwise, I think we'll wait a little while, Orrie. Until we can ask Miss Jennieveva what kind 'a folks the Stepneys are."

That night we found out. We went to meet Mama and sat on the steps of Miller's store with Philip Atterbury on his leash. That was my idea. I knew we shouldn't go inside—not on the first day Mama was working there, but I didn't see how sitting on the steps could rile Mr. Miller.

It wasn't quite so hot out under the broad porch of the mercantile store while we waited. Orrie was the first one to speak after we sat down. "Maybe we'll see Pa go by? Or the Duke or Grandpa?"

"Maybe," I answered her. Then I asked Wash straight out, "You saw Pa and the rest of them, didn't you?"

He didn't even try to lie to me. "I saw 'em, sure." Then he was quiet when I wanted him to keep on talking.

"How are they doing?" I asked him.

"Jim dandy. They like it fine at the Lion's Den. It's nice in there—nicer'n in our old bottle house."

"With rattlers under their pillows, Wash?"

"*They got pillows there!* We haven't got pillows at all."

That was true enough. We didn't have pillows. Pa had decided in San Bernardino that we could do without them.

"Pa comin' back? Is he givin' up yet?" asked Orrie.

"No," he told her. "He's already started workin' at the Silver Queen mine carpenterin'. The Duke got him the job."

"What about Grandpa?" I asked him.

"He's fine, too." He would have said something more, but right then Philip Atterbury started up barking. I thought maybe Pa or somebody our dog knew was coming, but no.

Instead a buggy, the fanciest dark green one I ever had seen, was going by down the ledge. A man in a top hat like Uncle Hiram's was handling the shiny sorrel mare. In the back under a canopy sat a yellow-headed lady in a pale green dress and flowery bonnet. There was a baby on her lap. Beside her was a girl a little bit younger than me. The buggy stopped in a cloud of pink dust right in front of us, and we watched as the girl climbed down and walked up the steps into Miller's.

She was something to see all right. Her dress was white with a pink sash and her shoes and stockings were white, too. Her eyes were blue as the Mojave sky and her long curls the color of fresh butter. Her straw bonnet was yellow with pink ribbons. She didn't stop to speak to us on the steps—not then. She did that later when she came out, sucking on a long piece of red-and-white peppermint.

"Who the devil are you?" she asked us then, standing over us. "When did you come here?"

I didn't like her language very much, but was polite to her just the same. "We're the Perkinses. We got here day before yesterday." I didn't give our whole names, figuring she was the kind who'd start laughing at us the way some folks did.

"I'm Belle Ann Stepney," she told me. Then she asked, "What does your father do?"

"He carpenters," Orrie told her.

She nodded, and said, "My father owns the Reba and the Ace of Hearts. They're mines."

"We know," came from Wash, who was staring at her openmouthed.

"I live up there." Belle Ann pointed to a big white

wooden house way up on the ledge, even bigger than Miss Jennieveva's place.

"We live in the bottle house," Wash boasted.

"I know that," Belle Ann told my brother. "I heard that some poor folks who didn't have a father had moved into it." She looked at Orrie's old dress and mine, and wrinkled up her nose. "You really are poor folks, aren't you?" she said. Then she added, "My father's very rich. He's a mine owner. I guess carpenters are poor, aren't they?"

"Yeah," Wash breathed at her. I wanted to kick him in the slats. I could tell by all the usual signs that he was falling in love with Belle Ann Stepney. Wash was in love a lot of the time with older girls. At nine he should have got over the habit.

"I've been to London, England, and Paris, France," said Belle Ann. "Don't you think that's interesting?" Then she sashayed back down the steps and into the buggy.

Although he was still barking his head off, she hadn't paid a bit of attention to Philip Atterbury. I didn't think that was very friendly of her, but then she hadn't been friendly to us at all.

"She didn't ask us once to come and play," said Orrie sadly, after the buggy had drawn away, leaving us in its dust.

"I don't think she does play," I told my sister. "She'd get her clothes dirty if she did." I kicked Wash now. "Close your mouth, Washington, before you catch a fly. The fairy princess's gone away in her punkin."

"Her pa must be awful rich," Orrie said, "if he can buy all that water to keep her wearin' white dresses up here."

"I guess all mine owners are," was what I said. "A lot richer'n we are." I felt sour about that old snob, Belle Ann. I hoped there was more than one Step-ney around our ages if Belle Ann was the way she was. Maybe another would be nicer. The baby didn't count. He was too little yet.

Mama wasn't mad to find us waiting when she came out. I guessed maybe she was too tired. She said her feet hurt her from standing up for nine hours. The first thing she did when we got home was unbutton her shoes and take off her stockings while I started up the fire and put the beans on to boil with a couple of smoked ham hocks in them.

"Callie," Mama complained to me, "I wish we could spare some water to put my feet in."

"We can, Mama," Orrie said. "Don't worry about the dinner dishes. Un Lung, he showed me how to use sand to clean 'em. It works better'n water."

Mama put her feet, then, in a half-full basin, sighed and closed her eyes, and said, "This feels wonderful. The work's not hard at Miller's, but oh my poor, poor feet!"

Just then we heard a knock at our door, a not very loud one. "Answer the door, Callie."

I went and opened it, and there stood Grandpa.

"Couldn't stand it no longer, honey," he told Mama, when he came inside. I wasn't sure if I should have let him in, but he got past me. He moved fast for an old man with rheumatism.

Mama opened her eyes, but didn't take her feet out of the water. "What was it that drove you out, Father?" she asked. "The food or the rattlesnakes—or the company?"

"None of 'em, honey. I missed you and the young 'uns. That was all. Gid and Hiram, they can get along without me. When I heard you was clerkin' at the mercantile store, I figured you needed me up here more'n them two did down there."

"You'll be glad to know, Father, that we are having beans for supper, too." Mama didn't laugh. I didn't see how she kept a straight face. I had to hide my laughing by pretending I was coughing. Grandpa Thompson sure didn't fancy beans much.

All the same he came across the room from the

door and plunked himself down on Mama's bed. Then he gazed all around him, and said, "I was here with Gid the other day, Hope, helpin' move you in. This place could use another room."

"It could," Mama agreed.

"Well, me and Cornelius will do it for you."

"Who's Cornelius, Grandpa?" Orrie piped up.

"Cornelius Twyford, that's who. He's Little Eva's husband. He was at the battle of Shiloh, too."

"This Little Eva, is she the lady who runs the biggest saloon here in Mojaveville, Father?" asked Mama.

"She sure does, Hope honey. She's a real nice lady. I told her all about you and Gid and Hiram. She knows you got troubles."

"The Duke of Kansas, you mean?" put in Mama, weary-sounding.

"Little Eva says you can have all the empty whiskey bottles you want. Me and Cornelius, we'll cart 'em up here and build you on a extra room, one for Wash and me."

"Pa ain't coming back?" demanded Wash.

"Nope, Gideon's adamant. You got to go back to him, Hope."

"What's that *adamant* mean?" I asked. The word was new to me, and I liked it.

"Hard like a rock, that's what. It's a word a professor told Gid. The professor's a minin' engineer—or used to be once. He lives at the Lion's Den."

"Well, when you see Gideon, tell him I'm adamant, too. He's got to come to us!" Mama sniffled, reached for a handkerchief in her apron pocket, and asked, "What do you and Mr. Twyford plan to do after you've added on to our magnificent house?"

"We're goin' prospectin' out in the desert, Cornelius and me."

"What about your rheumatism, Grandpa?" I'd noticed he'd been spry as all get out coming into our house.

"It's gettin' better. This desert air helps me, honey." He wiggled his shoulders. "Cornelius and me, we'll strike it rich out in the Mojave."

"Well, all right," said Mama. "You do as you please. The children and I, we'll get along fine." Then she added. "Just you see, Father, that you don't add any empty bottles at Little Eva's place. We can't afford that."

That sort of quieted all of us down. While Mama lay back, soaking her feet, I got busy and started using the riser Un Lung gave me and some flour, making us some bread. I guessed bread would come out all right, but I didn't see how I could ever bake a cake in Mojaveville except at night. The miners blasted out the mountain behind us all day long with powder, making tunnels. The whole ledge shook and trembled every twenty minutes. That blasting would make any cake fall in the oven.

4 ✳ New Folks

The month of May passed, getting hotter all the time.

Miss Jennieveva's bathtub came one afternoon late that month, and its arrival was the most important thing that happened that week. Slum Gullion Slim brought it in on his mud wagon. There it sat in the back, way up on top of a load of supplies for Miller's store. It was a great big claw-footed white

one that sparkled in the sunshine as if it were made
out of snow.

Slowly the mud wagon and mules came along the
ledge so folks could get a good view. I think everybody in Mojaveville who could stepped out to see it,
and because it was after six o'clock just about everybody who wasn't out prospecting was free to be
there. To celebrate, a couple of miners fired off six-
shooters; others cheered and hollered and waved
their hats in the air.

We stood on the porch of Miller's waiting for
Mama as usual, and we cheered it, too. Mama came
out along with Mr. Miller, a big old man with a
white walrus mustache; Mrs. Miller, who also was a
clerk, appeared with him.

I heard her say, sort of jealous, "Oh, so Jennieveva
Acheson's finally got her wish. She must be doin'
real well financially."

"Cost her a pretty penny, too," said Mr. Miller to
Mama. "All of thirteen dollars and eighty-five cents."

Mrs. Miller sniffed. "Miss Jennieveva must want a
bath pretty bad."

"Oh, no," Orrie told her. "Miss Jennieveva's the
best smellin' lady in town. She uses chypre. Callie
read the name on her perfume bottle, and it comes
all the way from Paris, France."

Mama gave Orrie a glance that should have told her to "shut up," but even if Orrie had said something else Mrs. Miller wouldn't even have heard it because of all the laughing. Right then somebody wearing a top hat popped up out of the bottom of Miss Jennieveva's bathtub where he'd been lying down, hiding.

"Hiram!" Mama exploded horror struck. "It's Hiram!"

"The Duke's the first one in her tub!" said Wash, just as if Uncle Hiram had done something wonderful instead of something terrible.

Orrie began to giggle. So did the Millers as Uncle Hiram went by in the mud wagon, smoking a big cheroot and waving and tipping his hat like a king to the miners, who were cheering louder than ever now.

Miss Acheson, of course, thought Uncle Hiram's arriving at her place in her bathtub a "disgusting thing," but not half as disgusting as when he rode up to her door, climbed out and down, and kissed her hand. She didn't snatch it away in time either, but she did nearly cut off his nose when she shut the door in his face.

Wash, Orrie, and I saw everything. We'd followed the mud wagon all the way to her place to see what she'd do. Philip Atterbury had gone along, too, and afterward he went up to Uncle Hiram and jumped on him. As Mama had said so many times, Philip Atterbury was "no judge of character."

"How's Pa, Uncle Hiram?" Wash had asked. I wanted to know this, myself, but I wouldn't ask the Duke of Kansas for anything. All the same I listened carefully.

"Gid? He's just fine." Uncle Hiram grinned at us. "How's sister Hope?"

"She's just fine, too. Tell Pa hello for Orrie and me," I said to him. Then I put my head up in the air, grabbed my sister by the hand, and started down the hill to Miller's again. I didn't give a darn that Wash and Philip Atterbury stayed behind.

The next day Uncle Hiram sent me a present, a chuckawalla lizard in a shoe box. Banjo brought it. I hated lizards and dumped it out behind our house and didn't even stay to see it run away. "This means I'm goin' to war with the Duke, too," I yelled at Banjo when he scooted off. "It won't just be Mama, it'll be me, too, California Perkins!"

"And me, too, Oregon Perkins!" came from Orrie.

"The Duke only wanted to give you a present." Banjo sounded hurt as he yelled at me from a safe distance. "He thought you'd like a chuckawalla."

"Well, I don't. And you tell the Duke of Kansas from me that I think he sent me a chuckawalla only because he couldn't find a gila monster with a poison bite." Just like Miss Acheson I went into the house and slammed the door on somebody's face—even if he was a hundred feet away.

Pa never came near us, but sent some money by Wash. I began to think as the days went by that he'd forgotten us.

June was really hot. Eph Miller told Mama "the first five years in the Mojave are the hottest." Mama had heard that lots of times by now, and so had I. We'd decided between us that a person got so weak after five years of the desert that he didn't care any-more how hot it was.

June was the month Miss Jennieveva caught Wash at it—showing folks up her back steps when she wasn't looking to let them see how fancy her bathtub was in her bathtub room. He was charging a penny a look and doing pretty well until she put a lock on the door and a stop to his money making. She told him she was "scandalized" at his behavior.

"Why?" said Wash to me after she'd scolded him. "It wasn't as if anybody was ever usin' it then."

Other interesting things happened that month. The Cornishmen came, five families at once; and we got to know more about Belle Ann and some other folks.

The Cornishmen, Mama said, were really English people. They came from a part of England called Cornwall, a place which was on the seacoast. They were miners by trade. A lot of the men up in Mojaveville weren't really miners at all to begin with. They were sailors or store clerks or butchers—all sorts of things, but they were born in the United States. Some of the younger Cornishmen had been born here, too, but all the same the Americans called them "foreigners," which they really weren't.

"Get back where you come from, Cousin Jack!" yelled a miner I knew lived with Pa and Uncle Hiram in the Lion's Den, as the Cornishmen came up the ledge in their wagons. Then he hee-hawed like a donkey and stuck his hands upon the sides of his head and wiggled them as if they were ears.

"Take your old Cousin Jenny with ya and all the little jacks and jennies. We don't want you up here!" shouted another miner, as the Cornishmen drove by.

Mama was standing with us when they came. Mr. Miller walked out onto his front porch too when he heard all the yelling.

I knew "jack" was a name for a male donkey and "jenny" for a female. I thought it was pretty insulting what the Cornishmen and their families got called.

"Why don't folks up here like those people, Mama?"

"I don't know." Mama shook her head.

"They're Cornishmen," explained Eph Miller. "Miners from Cornwall. American miners don't like 'em much."

"Why not?" I asked.

"Because they're sort of different, Callie. They stay to themselves wherever they go. They're better miners'n most, too." He lit a cheroot and went on, "I got nothing against 'em. They're good at paying their bills even if they are clannish. Folks say Cousin Jacks will work for less'n an American will and that seems to be true most places they go. Mine owners like to get miners cheaper—that's maybe why they're disliked." He turned and went back into his store, but not until he said to Mama, "Guess I better put in more flour stores and order out some saffron from Los Angeles."

"Saffron? What's that?" I asked Mama.

"A spice, Callie. I guess the Cornish people must use a lot of it."

Mama and I stood watching while the Cornishmen went by, noticing how the miners hooted at
them and how they glared back at the miners. Orrie
tugged at Mama's skirt, and said, "I counted ten
kids, Mama."

That's what I'd counted, too, ten new kids in
town.

Mama smiled at Orrie. "That's twelve school-age
children in all in Mojaveville—plenty for a school.
You see I was counting, too. I'll go see Miss Acheson
about it Sunday."

I went with Mama Sunday afternoon and sat
drinking tea with Miss Jennieveva in her front parlor, looking at the purple roses on her rug while she
and Mama talked. It seemed odd to me when I was
her houseworker to have tea with her, but it didn't
seem to bother anybody else a bit.

She nodded and nodded when she heard there
were at least twelve of us now of school age, then
said, "Mojaveville's going to be a city after all."

"It needs a school, Miss Acheson," put in Mama.
Then she added, "Edgar needs more education,
doesn't he? If he went to school, he'd free your
mornings."

I thought Mama'd put it pretty cleverly in case
Miss Jennieveva was lukewarm about the idea of

the school. But she wasn't. She put down her teacup next to her trailing plant, the one I had to dust the leaves of three times a week, and said, "Good idea, Mrs. Perkins, but I don't know as how the Cousin Jacks will take to it. They stick together in things, you know."

Mama had the answer to this problem. "They'd go to school if it was the law, wouldn't they?"

"Sure would," answered Miss Jennieveva.

I was right. Mama had figured it out all the way. "What we need, Miss Acheson, is a mayor and a council. They could make laws for Mojaveville."

Miss Jennieveva chewed this suggestion over, and after a while she said, "That ought to do the trick, Mrs. Perkins, I guess."

"Oh, it would," Mama told her. "You could start getting us a mayor right off."

Miss Jennieveva looked startled. "*Me?* How?"

"Well," said Mama, putting down her teacup, too. "You've got important men boarders and a bathtub. Would you share it with your boarders if you had plenty of water?"

"Of course. Costs me a fortune now to use it."

"Well, then." Mama took a deep breath. "Tell your boarders to get the town to elect a mayor and council who will raise tax money to sink a well in the desert, get a pump, build a reservoir up here, and put pipes into every house!" I gasped. Mama had sure thought it out all right.

The idea was so exciting that Miss Jennieveva's face got pink. "I can do it! I can do it, missus!" she said. "If they don't agree, I'll tell Un Lung to serve them lots more mashed spuds and skimp on the gravy. They don't like spuds dry."

"After we get water, the school will be the next thing we get out of the mayor and council, Miss Acheson."

"And I know what the third thing will be," put in Miss Jennieveva, breathless now. "A lending library. I always wanted one."

"Oh, Miss Jenieveva, you do think big!" said Mama, whose eyes were glistening.

I let them congratulate one another for a while, then I started in, not knowing if I'd be told to shut up. "Can I tell anybody, Belle Ann Stepney maybe, about the school?"

Miss Acheson shook her head. "No, Callie, for a while we have to work in the dark. If you take my advice, you won't pester the Stepneys at all. They're pretty stuck-up folks. Richer than is good for 'em. Been mine owners too long. They come here from Bodie with lots of money."

"So did you," I told her. I wished I could get to know Belle Ann, but I'd only seen her twice since the day she bought peppermint at the store, both times in the buggy. And both times Wash's mouth had hung open, admiring her. Belle Ann had seen us walking by or on Miller's steps, but she hadn't even nodded.

"So I did have some money," Miss Acheson answered, "but money never went to my head the way it did to Mrs. Stepney's."

That was true enough, I supposed, and white-dress Belle Ann certainly hadn't looked up us Perkinses.

"Shouldn't I try to make the Cornish girls welcome here, Miss Jennieveva?"

"The Cousin Jennies?" She sighed. "Well, you can try it, Callie, if you want to, but I don't think it'll do you much good. I doubt if you'll be able to understand half of what they're saying. They call us folks up here 'up alongs.' That means strangers, they tell me. It's mighty hard to get next to the Cousin Jacks and Jennies."

"But they *will* go to school?" Mama sounded anxious.

"They will—if the law says so. One thing you can say about 'em is that they're law-abiding folks."

* * *

That Sunday night was sure beautiful. When I went out to give Philip Atterbury an after-supper bone, I stood for a while to look at the stars. There wasn't any moon, and the sky was chockful of stars, millions of them, all shining brighter than anywhere else in the world, I guessed.

Because I was staring up at them so hard, I didn't see anyone coming, but I heard a foot scrape on the little crumbly rocks. When I swung around it was too dark to see the person's face. For a minute I was plenty scared, but then I noticed that Philip Atterbury hadn't barked once. Now he broke away from me and ran to the man, jumped up on him, and started whining.

"Hello, Callie, dear," said Pa.

"Hello, Pa." I wanted to run to him, like Philip Atterbury had, but I didn't. I had my pride.

"How're you girls? How're your ma and grandpa?" he asked me.

"Just fine," I said. "How're you?"

"Me, I'm fine, too."

Neither one of us said anything more until he turned around, then all he said to me was, "Good night, honey."

"Good night, Pa," I answered.

After Orrie and Wash had gone to bed and Grandpa, too, I told Mama what had happened. She didn't say a word, only sighed as she braided her hair for bed, then blew out the kerosene lamp.

"Mama." I just had to say something else to her. "Don't you go worrying too much over Pa. Wash, he keeps me posted on him. Pa ain't suff'rin' too much in the Lion's Den."

"California, that wasn't exactly what I was hoping to hear about him."

"Pa'll come home when he's good and ready," I said to her, comforting her.

Miss Jennieveva was true to her word and a fast worker to boot. Two weeks after Mama'd talked to her we had an election in Mojaveville, not the kind I liked with brass bands and fancy talkers, but a real quiet one. Eph Miller was elected mayor, and then Mr. Stepney, a couple of miners I didn't know, and two of Miss Acheson's boarders were elected to the city council. That was the first big step toward getting Mojaveville a school.

"You tell your mama for me that the next step shouldn't be rushed too fast, Callie. We'll take care of the water trouble first, then the school. After that the lendin' library," Miss Acheson told me.

Right away a well got sunk and a big wooden reservoir was started up on the hill above the mines.

Wash said Pa worked on the reservoir. I used to listen sometimes to the hammering up there before I started out to work in the morning. It made me feel comfortable somehow, to know that water was on the way and that Pa was up there and could maybe look down and see us kids going back and forth to Miss Acheson's.

I gave up completely on Belle Ann Stepney after a while. She kept going by all the time in her pa's fancy rig, but she never got out of it or asked us to play. If that was the way she wanted to act, I wasn't going to call on her or let Orrie or lovesick Wash go either.

Orrie and me did go spying on the Cornish families a little bit, though. They sure built funny houses, blasting out sides of the canyon and putting up lean-tos in front of the holes they made. At that they probably weren't any funnier than our old bottle house, which Mr. Twyford and Grandpa were still to add on to.

I'd met Mr. Twyford and his wife, Eva, too. She really was tiny, a little like the heroine in *Uncle Tom's Cabin,* with yellowish gray hair and blue eyes. She was old, though, older'n Miss Jennieveva, as old as Grandpa even, and she wore bright silk dresses with big bustles on 'em. She came to meet us

at the back door of her saloon once. I liked her because she said Philip Atterbury was handsome.

"You're handsome, too, mam. Your hair's just the
color his is," Orrie told her.

That made her smile with pleasure all right,
though kind of thinly. I hoped the compliment
would make her save bottles faster. We sure needed
that new room bad.

Mr. Cornelius, her husband, was a nice man. He
had white whiskers, not gray like Grandpa's, long
hair like Buffalo Bill's, and he always wore a gray
suit. In red he would have made a good Saint
Nicholas. He had a soft way of talking, one I never
had heard before. He said he came from West Virginia. Grandpa was thick with him because Cornelius had been in the Mexican War and Civil War
both, and in particular because he'd been at Shiloh,
too. He'd been a prospector for a long, long time out
in the California deserts, though he'd never hit a big
bonanza yet. He knew all there was to know about
prospecting but Grandpa said he didn't know much
about saloon keeping, which was why Little Eva
did that work.

Late in June Cornelius and Grandpa started hauling up bottles in wheelbarrows and adding on our
room. I didn't get to watch them put it up, because

they worked only in the mornings, when I worked, too. In the afternoons nobody worked outside at all during the summer. It was too hot for that. About all anyone could do was sit around and breathe. Mama, Orrie, and me, we wore calico all the time and as few petticoats as we could get by with. It was a lucky thing Mama was skinny. As she told me, "My corsets would kill me up here."

The first week of July, just before they set off a lot of blasting power to celebrate the Fourth and blew out one of Miss Acheson's parlor windows, Orrie and I went to visit some of the Cornishmen. We'd picked out the family we wanted to get to know, the one that had girls our ages. Mama had waited on the parents at Miller's and said they were nice folks, once you got on to what they wanted to say. Their name was Trewhiddle, Mr. and Mrs. Piran Trewhiddle. Mama found out the names of their girls were Gennys and Columba. Their baby brother was named Arthur. At least, we'd heard of that name.

We left Wash at home to take care of Philip Atterbury. Maybe Cornish people didn't like dogs. A lot of the people in Mojaveville didn't seem to take to ours, in spite of what the Duke of Kansas had put in his letter. Wash thought it was because Philip Atterbury wasn't very good looking, but I guessed it was because he growled a lot and acted like a biter, even though he wasn't. He was a bluffer.

When we got to the Cornishmen's place, I knocked at the door of the lean-to, hoping a kid would answer, but instead out came an old man with whiskers to his waist

"*Meea navidna cowzasawzneck*," he said, or at least that's what I thought he said.

A kid, the one Orrie's age, popped her head out right beside him then. I knew from what Mama'd said that she was Columba. "My granfer, he don't speak English," she told us.

"What'd he just say?" I asked her.

"He said, 'I don't speak English.' "

"But you *are* English!" I couldn't believe her.

Columba, who was dark haired, shook her head. "No, we be Cornish. Cornish ain't English. Who're you?"

I was so flustered I said, "Me, I'm California Perkins," instead of saying Callie, the way I usually do.

"Why're you called California?" She didn't laugh.

" 'Cause I was born here. Why're you called Columba?"

"I was born here, too. I'm called Columba 'cause it's Cornish. Your name doant zeem fitty to me."

I really didn't know what that meant, but I let it pass. "Do you want to play?" I asked her. "You and your sister?"

Granfer had disappeared by now. The older girl I knew was Gennys had taken his place. Gennys was dark haired, too, with an olive-colored skin and short nose. She said. "I dun't feel so very clever now."

"She don't look it neither," whispered Orrie, who didn't know yet that this meant Gennys wasn't feeling "well." Neither did I.

"If I wasn't clever, I sure wouldn't tell folks," put in my sister, who had the giggles by now.

"The poor *shamick* up-along *edder zackly*," said Columba to Gennys, then she shook her head from side to side.

I guessed what this head shaking meant. They thought Orrie was crazy.

"She ain't crazy at all! If that's why you're shaking your head," I exploded. Then I grabbed Orrie by the hand, and we left the old Trewhiddle's house. Now I knew what Mama and Miss Jennie-veva had meant about Cornish people being hard to understand. I couldn't see what Mama had in mind, though, when she said the Trewhiddles were nice folks. Maybe Mr. and Mrs. Trewhiddle were. Gennys and Columba were awful.

"They didn't like us at all," Orrie complained, as we walked home, the sun beating down on us.

"They didn't understand us," I told her.

"They understood *us* all right. We just couldn't understand *them*." Orrie was bawling. "They didn't want to. We ain't got any friends in Mojaveville, Callie. That Belle Ann's a snob, a bad old snob who wears white dresses 'cause she's rich. Wash, he's got Pa and the Duke and Un Lung and Banjo." She stuck her fists into her eyes. "And you and me, we ain't got nobody."

"Sure, we do." I agreed with her really, but it would only make her feel worse to let her know it. "We got each other, and we got Mama and Miss Jennieveva and a lady teacher comin' this fall."

"Old ladies ain't no fun. What I want is a kid!"

We stood in the middle of the street as the ore wagons rattled by us, spreading pink dust all over us. "Orrie, a teacher'll take the starch out of stuck-up Stepney and she'll fix old Gennys and Columba. She'll teach the Cornishers good English. She'll take care of Banjo Acheson, too. She'll teach him to talk about somethin' else other'n Wyatt Earp and gunmen and no good people like that."

I put my arm around Orrie and led her home. "Just you wait and see!"

5 ✳ Disasters

The rest of July Orrie and me kept to ourselves after we finished work.

"The dickens with the Stepneys and the Cousin Jennies," was what Orrie said to me.

I agreed.

We told Miss Jennieveva how bad the Trewhiddles had treated us. She said not to pay it any mind. Cornish people were just plain queer and there was no telling how they'd take to things. Whatever, it wouldn't be the way anybody'd expect.

On the thirtieth of July a doctor came to Mojaveville, our very first one. On the thirty-first everybody in town knew the bad news about him. He was a drinker. Little Eva had him thrown out of her saloon into the street that day. There he was, his big face all red, lying in the dust on his back singing a song all to himself when Miss Acheson walked by from Miller's. I was with her, carrying some groceries home for her in a basket.

"Hullo, my love," he said to her, rolling over toward her and tipping his hat, blocking our way.

"Good afternoon," she told him, then stepped around him fast, as I did. I could tell by the way she snorted that she didn't like him.

"I didn't know you knew the doctor, Miss Jennieveva."

"Good gracious, child, you don't think that I know that besotted beast, do you?" She stopped in her tracks and gave me a shocked look.

"You said good afternoon to him!"

She shuddered. "I had to say something, didn't I? Well, Callie, the only thing I know about that creature is that he found his own level of company in the Lion's Den. He's living there, I hear tell. I'm grateful he didn't come up to my place."

I put in, "He'll get sunstroke maybe bein' out in the street that way." I felt I ought to tell her. It wouldn't be right to let him loll out there and die.

"It wouldn't be any great loss, Callie. This town needs a doctor, a sober one. Heaven help anyone who breaks a leg or catches a fever. I doubt if he knows a cure for any ailment except a big dose of what he drinks." Miss Jennieveva went on. "Don't worry about him, Callie. He'll be picked up soon and hauled off by somebody from the Lion's Den. That's one thing you can say about that terrible hole. The people there look after their own."

What she said was true. I heard later on from Wash that Uncle Hiram came by and spotted the doctor in the street. He borrowed a wheelbarrow from Mr. Cornelius, dumped the doctor into it, and took him home.

Mama was horrified when she heard about Mojaveville's doctor. "He's always drinking, day and night," she told Grandpa once. "Folks who come into Miller's say he's a disgrace to his profession. Mrs. Miller thinks he ought to be run out of town on a rail—if not tarred and feathered. They say he'll murder his first patient."

"He set up in practice yet, honey?" Grandpa asked.

"No, he hasn't been sober long enough to get an office and put out a shingle."

"Maybe he won't practice at all. Maybe he just come up here for a vacation. If he don't practice, what he does is his own business, Hope."

Mama laughed, wiped her wet forehead with her apron and went on stirring our corned-beef stew. It was hot as Hades in the desert in August. Standing near our stove was enough to make me want to drop. "I'd give a year of my life for one little lump of ice, Father," she said. "Let's not discuss the doctor anymore. It's too hot to get mad."

It went up past 110 degrees every day the first week in August. The heat made living hard and folks bad tempered. It didn't help much when I complained to have Miss Jennieveva tell me again that the first five years are the hottest. I didn't think I'd ever get used to the heat, but I quit bellyaching about it. Keeping my mind on it only made me hotter. The nights weren't so bad. We opened our door and windows, then, and let in the air, a thing Mama and Grandpa agreed on. They couldn't de-cide what to do in the daytime. Grandpa said open the house for the breezes, and Mama said no, keep it shut up tight to keep the night coolness in. Grandpa's way we got flies. Mama's way it was a bake oven by noon and Philip Atterbury's tongue hung out so far when he sagged himself down on the floor that I almost stepped on it.

On the night of the ninth we had a special treat, half a watermelon. Some Indians had come up with them from the Colorado River to the east. Mama had splurged and bought it for us. It wasn't ice-cold, the way it should be, but all the same it was wonderful.

"I ain't never going to wash my face again," Wash said. "That's so I can go on tastin' watermelon forever when I lick it with my tongue."

Orrie giggled, and said, "That's a better excuse than you gen'rally have for not washin'."

I asked Mama, "When's the water coming to town?"

Grandpa answered while Mama went on crocheting. "Pretty soon, Callie. There's been a couple loads 'a pipe wagoned in already, and they're settin' up a pump down by the well."

"That'll be a big day, won't it?"

"It sure will, honey girl, even if nobody celebrates it with fireworks." He winked at me. "Maybe Cornelius and me will strike it rich, and we'll have a bathtub, too, a gold one."

Wash scowled. We'd been bathing Saturday nights

in just a quart of water each. He liked it fine. I never got the soap off proper, and I itched in some places.

"Nope, if I strike it rich, we'll move out'a here to a mansion, one of adobe and wood."

"*If* you strike it rich, Father!" Mama put her crochet hook and thread away and went to stand at the door of our house, where she looked out down on Mojaveville.

Lamps were shining soft yellow in every house and tent. A coyote was singing to a quarter moon and one star. The desert wind was blowing some, but not stirring up much dust. It was a pretty night. Even the saloon piano pounders were playing soft tunes that sounded pretty too.

I knew Mama was thinking about Pa. She always was when she got that faraway listening look on her face. I wished we could all be together again. I guessed Orrie did, too.

At midnight that night somebody knocked on our door. I heard Mama get up and so I got up, too. I came and stood in the dark behind her. I couldn't see who she was talking to, but all the same I knew who it was. It had to be Mrs. Trewhiddle. "Missus," she said to Mama, "Columba and my Arthur, they not be so clever." Mrs. Trewhiddle sounded worried.

"They're sick, you mean? What's wrong with them?" Mama asked.

"Hot, missus. They be hot and cough."

"Do their throats hurt, Mrs. Trewhiddle?"

"Aye, missus. Columba, she does. I done all I could. We all did."

Mama must have heard me come up. She spoke to me over her shoulder. "Callie, you get dressed and go down to the Lion's Den and get that doctor up here right away." Then she turned up the lamp and spoke to Mrs. Trewhiddle. "You go back home, dear. Keep the children warm and in bed. I'll be down as soon as I can."

When Mrs. Trewhiddle went away, Mama talked some more to me. Her face looked as grim as her words. "It could be diphtheria, Callie. I pray to the Lord it isn't. I went through that once before in a mining camp. It was a nightmare."

I was throwing on my clothes all the time she talked to me about diphtheria. I knew about that awful disease, all right. They'd had it in Sacramento, too, and lots of kids there died from it. A couple of them had been in my grade at school.

"If that doctor's been drinking, Callie, we're going to have to sober him up. I'll have the coffee ready when you get back. Have Pa or Hiram help you."

I was a little bit scared of going to the Lion's Den,

a place I'd never been to, but all the same I went, taking Philip Atterbury along with me for protec-tion. When I knocked on its door, a man I'd never seen before came out. "Who you lookin' for, little girl?"

"For the doctor," I told him.

The stranger laughed. "He's passed out."

"Well, then, would you bring out Mr. Gideon Perkins or Mr. Hiram Perkins?"

"Can't get Gideon," he said. "He's sound asleep. The Duke of Kansas, he's in the middle of a poker game."

"Please, mister, get the Duke. Tell him it's Callie who wants to see him."

In a few minutes Uncle Hiram came out. The first thing he said was, "What you doin' out here at this hour?"

"Mama sent me," I explained. "She didn't really want you. She wants the doctor."

"Somebody sick up at your place?" he asked me quickly.

"No, but Mama thinks maybe there's diphtheria in the camp."

He whistled. "I'll get the doc all right, but he ain't in no good condition."

"Mama guessed that. I think she's making coffee."

I added, "I'm sorry to take you away from your poker game, Uncle Hiram."

"Don't matter a hill of beans to me, Callie. I was winnin'. That's a good time to get out of it."

He went back into the Lion's Den while I waited. I was glad I didn't have to go inside. It sure wasn't any place for ladies. Now and then I got a little whiff of it—cheroots and whiskey, that's what it smelled of. Our dog didn't like it either. He sneezed.

The doctor smelled the same when the Duke brought him out. He was walking, but just barely. Uncle Hiram had a good grip on him, though, and got him up to our house all right with me following on behind, carrying his heavy doctor's bag. The doctor was a pretty good singer. I learned all the words of "Beautiful Dreamer" from him as we went along.

Mama was ready with the coffee when Uncle Hiram dragged the doctor through the door and steered him to a chair. He didn't look good. His hair, what he had of it, was a mess, and he didn't have on a cravat or vest, not even a coat, nothing but his shirt and trousers, and they weren't clean.

"Hiram," said Mama, "you have yourself a cup of coffee and get him to have one, too, if you have to pour it down him. We better hurry."

"I'll wake the doc up fast," said the Duke of Kansas.

Mama turned to me. "You go get Miss Jennieveva up. Tell her what's happened. Tell her we might have to send for her and to be ready."

I scooted out the door again with Philip Atterbury and went down to the boarding house, our dog barking all the way. Then I pounded on that door, too. Banjo answered me after I'd done a lot of knocking. He was half asleep. "What you want here, Callie?" Although he was plenty sleepy he could still scowl good in the lamplight at me.

"Mama sent me. Please get Miss Jennieveva up, Edgar. Please hurry."

"Why?"

"Because folks are sick."

"Who's sick?"

"Columba Trewhiddle and her brother."

He made a face. "The Cousin Jacks, they ain't people. Send for a horse doctor for them."

I felt like saying, "If that's the way you think, I don't think you're people either," but I didn't. Instead I told him, "You listen good to me, Banjo. If you don't get Miss Acheson up, I'll tell on you in the morning that you wouldn't do what Mama wanted. Miss Jennieveva'll fix you."

He took the lamp up, said "squaw" to me and went away. After a long time he came back—alone though. He looked worried now. "She can't come. She's sick; she says she's got a fever."

"Sore throat, too?" I asked him.

He nodded.

I was really scared now. I didn't stop to tell Banjo what I was scared of. I headed to home fast as I could with Philip Atterbury running by my side.

The doctor had his eyes all the way open now. Mama was standing over him with the coffeepot in her hand, ready to pour some more, while Uncle Hiram sat in our second chair.

"Mama," I burst in with, "Miss Jennieveva, she's sick too."

"What symptom's she got?" asked the doctor. His voice sounded different from when he'd been sing-ing "Beautiful Dreamer."

"Same as Columba has," was my answer.

"Hmm," came from him, "and that Acheson woman's as old as the hills. Hmm!"

"Are you ready to go, Aubrey?" asked the Duke.

Aubrey, which I guessed was the doctor's first name, ran his hand over his head and face, and said, "Guess I'm as ready as I'll ever be, Hiram."

"We better leave then," Mama told him. "Hiram,

thank you. We won't need you anymore. You can go back to your game now."

"All right, Hope. Call me if you need me—even if I ain't no great shakes with sick folks."

She nodded, picked up her shawl, and out we went, the doctor bringing up the rear. We hurried down the ledge to the Trewhiddles. Mrs. Trewhiddle was at the door of their lean-to with a lamp.

"How are they?" asked Mama.

"Not so clever, missus."

Mama swung around to face me. "Callie, you stay here. Even if you're almost thirteen, I don't want you in there in case it's diphtheria. I may need you to run more errands for me."

I knew what she meant all right. That disease was hardest on real little kids mostly, but it could be dangerous for me, too. I didn't want to go inside Trewhiddles'.

I stood outside and waited and waited. Pretty soon I went to sit on a big outcrop of rock a few feet away from the door. I waited some more. Finally Mama came out with a lantern. She told me with a sigh. "Thank the Lord, it's not diphtheria, Callie. Dr. Aubrey thinks it's la grippe. That's bad enough though."

I knew what that was. Sometimes folks died of

this disease, too. "Then that's what Miss Jennie-veva's got?" I asked.

"Most likely, Callie. Now you go get Eph Miller up and get a big bottle of vinegar and a pound of butter and six onions—big ones. I'm going to make a batch of cough syrup. La grippe makes bad coughs."

"Miller's has got Cherry Pectoral, Mama."

"This is better. Now you get along with you."

Well, I got the Millers up and got the things Mama wanted, told them there was la grippe in the camp, and left. When I got back to Trewhiddles', Mama made me come inside and start making onion juice in a ricer. I got a good look at the Cornish folks' house before I started crying so hard from onions that I couldn't see anymore. Mr. Trewhiddle had blasted out a pretty big place with a kitchen parlor in front and a curtained-off place in back. They had more furniture than we did, a rocking chair, too. Beside the rocking chair was a cradle. There was a baby in it, coughing, when he wasn't crying. Mama picked him up sometimes while I fixed onions and walked back and forth with him, patting him on the back.

"Where's the doctor?" I asked her.

"Gone up to Miss Acheson's. He's done what he can down here. He says he'll be back soon." She jerked her head toward the curtain. "Dolly's with Columba."

"Who's Dolly?"

"Mrs. Trewhiddle."

"Oh. How's Gennys?" I asked.

"She's all right. She and her father aren't here. They went over to the Boscawens' next door."

"How's Columba?"

"Not very well, Callie."

I went on ricing onions, sniffling, with tears running down my face. Sometimes Columba coughed, as if she was strangling, in the back part of the house. She sounded awful.

"When you're done," Mama told me, "heat up the juice and the stuff you brought with some salt. We should have boiled the onions slowly, but there isn't time. This way'll have to do."

While the baby Arthur cried and Columba went on coughing, I mixed the onion syrup and got it boiling. It thickened up right off.

"It's ready, Mama," I told her. "Should I let it cool?"

She put the baby back in his cradle, then came up to me while he went on wailing and waving his little fists in the air. Mama took the big spoon from me, tasted the syrup, and nodded. "It's just fine. I'll pour some out to cool for the baby. Columba, she's old enough to take it hot." Mama put syrup in two cups and then took one and went behind the curtain. She called out to me, "You hold the baby, Callie."

I'd never held a baby before. I was nervous about it, but I picked him up and held onto him all right. He was awful hot to the touch. He didn't wiggle at all, and he'd stopped crying just before I picked him up. I looked down at his face. It had been really red when Mama had held him, but now it wasn't any more. It was getting bluish, and he was gasping as if he couldn't get his breath.

"Mama! Mama!" I yelled. "He's turnin' color!"

She came flying through the curtains, grabbed the baby away from me, and shoved me toward the door. "Hurry! Hurry. Find that doctor and get him back here."

I found him halfway down the road to the Trewhiddles'. "The baby! It's the baby, doctor!" I shouted at him before I got up to him. "Mama sent me for you!"

We both headed back, running to the lean-to. There the doctor took the baby from Mama, looked at him, did something I couldn't see to the baby's face, and with a deep sigh put him back in his little cradle. The doctor's face sagged the same way his shoulders did.

"He's dead, Mrs. Perkins," he said quietly to

Mama. "There wasn't a thing in the world anyone could have done for the little feller. La grippe's like that." He straightened up now and told us, "There's three more cases of it up at the boarding house. I think we've got an epidemic on our hands."

Mama wiped her eyes with a fold of her skirt. She sounded weary when she spoke to me. "You go on home, Callie. The doctor and I, we'll do what we have to do here. On the way you stop at the Lion's Den and tell Hiram to tell Gid it's la grippe. I think I'm going to be here all night. In the morning you tell your grandpa, too. You and he make up some cough syrup." A tear rolled down her cheek before she could catch it. "I'll go tell Dolly now about her baby."

I couldn't go before I asked the question worry-ing me. "Mama, how's Columba? She going to die, too?"

Mama shook her head. "No, I don't think so. Co-lumba seems to be a pretty strong little girl."

After that I did go home. Because I was crying about the baby's dying I didn't walk so fast. I was remembering how he'd gasped for air and how little he was and how his face had looked. But I got to the Lion's Den all right, and Pa, who was up now, walked me home. I told him about the Cornish baby dying.

"Yes, Callie," he said, as we went along. "I know how it is. We lost a little boy once, too, your mama and me."

That pulled me up short. "I didn't know that, Pa!"

"It ain't exactly the sort of thing you go around talking to folks about. He was born before you were —only lived a couple 'a hours." Pa didn't say any-thing more.

"What did you and Mama name him—my brother?"

"He would 'a been Edward, Edward Gideon."

"Oh." There didn't seem to be any more to say.

Pa wanted to talk about him, though. "Happened a long time ago, honey. Babies, little kids—it's hard to bring 'em up in minin' camps."

"Is that maybe why Mama hates Mojaveville so much, Pa?"

It was a lot lighter now, getting on toward dawn. East over the desert I could see some pale yellow color in the sky, enough to make out Pa's face by. He looked older to me and he needed to shave.

"I guess so, Callie," he told me. "You kids take care of yourselves. La grippe, it's a bad one."

"We will," I promised him. Then I added, "Pa, I won't tell Orrie or Wash about Edward Gideon."

"Do what you think's the best thing. You're pretty near grown up now," he said to me. He turned away, and I stood at the door of our bottle house looking after him. I wished he'd come inside and stay. I was sure tired of having our family split up. We were lonesome without Pa.

The epidemic went on for a whole three weeks. Half the camp, it seemed to me, came down with la grippe. Wash caught it and so did Un Lung, but they weren't babies or old folks, so they weren't sick very long. Grandpa took care of Wash, and we all worried over him while we poured the onion syrup down him. Un Lung had lots of cousins in China-town to look after him. Miss Jennieveva didn't have it so good, though. She was older and she was in bed a long time. She fretted a lot because she didn't know what was going on in the kitchen, where one of Un Lung's relatives had taken over. Too, three of her boarders were still flat on their backs. Banjo and Orrie and me, we fetched and carried for all four of them when we weren't doing our regular work. By the time the epidemic was over I weighed two pounds lighter on Mr. Miller's feed scales and was pretty tuckered out. The old Stepneys didn't get sick. They went to San Bernardino and stayed away all the time la grippe was in Mojaveville.

Mama kept busy day and night nursing alongside

Doctor Aubrey once she found out Wash was going to be all right. Mr. Miller went on paying her, just as if she was working, saying that nurses were more important than store clerks in epidemics. We thought he was sure nice. Doctor Aubrey and Mama taught a couple of the Cornish women how to look after sick folks, too. I was proud of Mama, who'd made friends left and right for us in Mojaveville by her nursing. She didn't get sick, though we all worried about her all the time.

The doctor didn't get sick either, nor did Uncle Hiram. Folks said that was because la grippe germs couldn't compete with old whiskey fumes. Mrs. Gideon Perkins was a saint, people told me in the street, an absolute saint. I didn't say anything to them, even though Mama was mighty quick with a slap sometimes. She didn't have red hair for nothing.

While la grippe was in Mojaveville, the doctor didn't do any drinking. But when it was over, he went on a real tooting bender that lasted for five days. Then he sort of swore off, only drinking after six o'clock at night. He finally put up his shingle on Main Street. Folks started to come to him now that he'd proved himself as a doctor and spruced himself up a little. He hadn't saved all of his patients.

Twenty people had died, and we had a cemetery. But nobody held his not saving everybody against him. He'd done the best he could, so folks thought he was a good-enough doctor.

Miss Jennieveva became interested in him now that he was a little bit reformed. "He a bachelor, Callie?" she asked me the first day she got up out of bed.

"I dunno, Miss Acheson."

"You ask your Mama for me."

I promised and I did. Mama didn't know. When I told Miss Jennieveva, she sounded shocked. "What, your mama and the doctor worked side by side days at a time getting folks well, and she doesn't know that about him!"

"No, mam, she says they didn't talk much except about la grippe."

"Um," came from Miss Jennieveva. "I'll bet Dr. Aubrey is a bachelor. He looks to me like he carries a secret sorrow."

I didn't agree. If he was grieving for something, I suspected it was for all the whiskey he just gave up. But I didn't say a thing. It seemed to me that Miss Acheson was setting her cap for the doctor, but I doubted if it'd do her much good. And it didn't either—no matter how many times she had him up to dinner when Un Lung was back in her kitchen. I told Orrie, "I guess she'll have to go to Frisco and buy one after all."

Mama got busy again on the school as soon as she was rested up from working so hard during la grippe. She was popular now with the Cornish people, especially the women, and she easily got them interested in the idea of a school. Then she came to see Miss Jennieveva for tea again on a Sunday afternoon late in August. I tagged along, too.

"Water's being piped in next week, Miss Jennieveva," said Mama.

"So I heard tell," came from Miss Acheson, who offered me a cookie.

"It's high time we had a school board," Mama said. "Have you talked to the mayor about it?"

"Yes, I have. He says he'll call a council meeting and they'll appoint a school board. The board'll hire a teacher from Los Angeles first thing."

Miss Jennieveva nodded. "Schoolhouse can come later. Mojaveville will have to vote the money to build it."

"There's a mine shaft where school can start maybe," Mama said to her. "The Reba mine, it's worked out, I heard. My father's been in it. He said the tunnel's an even seventy degrees all year."

Miss Acheson sighed. It had gone up to 112 degrees by noon that day. "That cool? Makes me want to go back to school, too. Well, Mrs. Perkins, I'll start in on my boarders at dinner tonight about this bus'ness of a school."

Three days later two terrible things happened in Mojaveville.

Philip Atterbury got loose—really loose this time. Wash didn't tie his rope tightly enough to the leg of Grandpa's bed, and in the middle of the night he got loose and nosed open the front door. After that there was no stopping him getting away.

We hunted for him and asked questions about him and whistled for him all over the ledge, but nobody'd seen hide or hair of him.

"He's prob'ly gone out in the desert to keep the coyotes comp'ny," Grandpa told us.

Wash had a broken heart and was crying. "He won't never come back."

"That dog ain't got the sense to find his way back," Grandpa muttered.

"Philip Atterbury'll leave his bones to bleach out there." Sometimes my sister thought up the strangest things to say.

"Oh, well, we'll get us another hound in Burdoo

next time we go there—a pup this time," Grandpa promised her and Wash to calm them down.

"And we'll raise him up *right!*" said Orrie.

Philip Atterbury had come to us out of nowhere in Sacramento. He was full grown then, and I guessed he had been running away from some other family.

"And Callie won't name him either this time!" Wash added, glowering at me as if it was my fault our dog ran away.

The other terrible thing was that the mayor and the council went crazy. Or that's what Mama claimed.

They put Uncle Hiram on the school board.

6 * Miss Dorothea

Miss Jennieveva was as mad as Mama—if not madder. "The Duke of Kansas on the school board!" she exploded in my face, when she heard the news. "Might as well put that cur dog of you folks on it."

"He's gone—run away, Miss Acheson." I didn't think it was fair the way she picked on Philip Atterbury. After all, he hadn't gone riding through town

in her bathtub. She had a right to be mad with
Uncle Hiram, but not our poor old dog who was
lying somewhere out on the Mojave bleaching his
bones.

I didn't talk to her about anything except the
water coming in after that—that and how nice it'd
be not to have to send her sheets to Barstow now.
"Your boarders will be tickled to be clean again,
won't they, Miss Jennieveva?" I said to her once.

She gave me a look that could kill chickens.
"Callie, what do you mean—'clean'?"

"Sheets once a week instead of four. Un Lung's
relations can do 'em up here now."

"You go see if Un Lung wants any supplies," she
ordered me. "If he wants anything from Miller's,
you go along there with your brother."

I guessed I was being got rid of. "Did I say something wrong, Miss Jennieveva?"

"Yes, you did, California Perkins. You told me
that I don't keep a clean boardin' house."

"But you do. I help clean it up. I ought to know."

"Callie," she said, "I know that sheets ought to be
changed every week. If I could have afforded to
have mine changed more often, I would have."

I thought for a minute. Yes, I supposed I hadn't
been very nice, so I told her, "I'm sorry. I didn't

mean to hurt your feelings. I guess I didn't think before I opened my mouth."

Miss Jennieveva laughed and sat down. "Just realizing that's the beginning of growing up, really growing up, my dear." She took my hand for a minute, then let it go. "You know, Callie, some folks never do learn that—not to open their mouths and say everything they have on their minds without doing any thinking about whether they ought to or not. I forgive you."

All the same I went with Wash on a punishment-in-the-heat errand to Miller's, and when I got there I waited till Mama was finished measuring off some curtain yardage for one of the Cornish ladies. Then I asked, "Mama, is it true, some folks never do grow up?"

"Who told you that?"

"Miss Acheson."

Mr. Miller, the mayor, had overheard me. "It's true, California."

"I don't think my Uncle Hiram ever did." I looked the mayor right in the eye, and asked him, "Mr. Miller, why'd you put him on the school board?"

"Well, dear," he said to me, hauling a piece of horehound candy out of the big glass jar in front of him and giving it to me, "it was because we thought we needed a fresh point of view."

"The Duke's got *that?*" I couldn't help but ask, even if Mama was glaring at me behind his back. Then I said, "Thanks."

"You got to admit that there isn't really anyone quite like your Uncle Hiram here in Mojaveville," went on the mayor.

"There sure ain't." In spite of Mama's signaling me to "shut up" I went on. "He thinks a old bachelor's nature's most noblest creature." I was done talking now so I put the candy in my mouth.

Mayor Miller laughed. "Up here that's a fresh point of view, Miss Perkins. Just about all we got in Mojaveville is unwilling bachelors."

Gennys and Columba Trewhiddle came up to play with us without being asked the day after the water pipes got put up in our house. We weren't mad at them anymore, so we were nice to them. Besides, we felt sorry about their losing their baby brother.

It was on a Saturday, and all we could talk about was how everybody in Mojaveville would be cleaner Sunday morning. Grandpa had bought us a big copper washtub at Miller's and a bar of yellow soap. The washtub sat there by our stove glittering in the sunshine that came through the yellow bottles as if it were made of gold.

Wash and Banjo, they'd left town early that day for the desert. "My brother, he's out in the Mojave grievin' 'cause we got us a bathtub," Orrie told Columba. "He told Mama once in Sacramento when he was getting a bath, 'Kill me, kill me, but don't wash my neck!'"

Gennys nodded. She handled English better'n Columba did. "Boys is like that. They don't like to wash their skins. That's the way the Nanfan boys is."

I didn't know the Nanfans, but I'd seen 'em all right. They were tall sort of dusty-haired boys who never seemed to notice Orrie and me when we walked past them on Main Street. They wouldn't even talk to Wash and Banjo.

"We know a lady who's got a real bathtub, a white one," Orrie put in, being friendly. "Even the old Stepneys haven't got that."

"Who'd they be?" asked Gennys, ignoring Miss Jennieveva's bathtub.

"Rich folks. Stuck-up rich folks. They was here before even we got here," explained my sister.

"There's a girl Stepney, Belle Ann," I told Gennys.

"We're gonna punch her in the eye the day school starts up." Orrie looked at me, and I shook my head, but all the same she said, "Maybe Callie won't do it, but I'm going to."

"You make her *scritch* like a *whitneck?*" asked Columba, eager as all get out.

"Yell like a weasel," Gennys told us was what she meant.

"Just like a old weasel," Orrie agreed.

Well, we got on fine after that and learned lots of interesting things from Gennys and Columba—like King Arthur's castle being in Cornwall, and that Cornish miners mined way out under the sea in copper mines half a mile deep and heard waves breaking over their heads. Cornishmen, who'd been mining in Cornwall for at least a thousand years, believed fairies lived in mines, fairies who were called knockers. Knockers were only as big as one-year-old babies, but they were dangerous all the same. They hated whistling and the sign of the cross, but they were friendly if somebody left bread crumbs for them. Gennys told us that Mojaveville's silver mines had knockers, plenty of them. Her pa and Mr. Nanfan had heard 'em in the tunnels. That gave Orrie and me the shivers all right.

That day Orrie and I went back to Trewhiddles' for tea and had "thunder and lightning," buttered cakes with syrup and canned milk on them. We learned, too, what the Cornishmen used saffron for—their pasties, pies they made with bacon and turnips. I was slow drinking my tea so Mrs. Tre-

whiddle told me to "haste and gaddle it" and then
we'd better "go up along." I guessed this meant to
drink up and go home, so we did.

I told Grandpa Thompson about our new friends.
"They're sort of diff'rent, but they're nice. Next time
we go, Mrs. Trewhiddle's going to give us mugwort
tea instead of plain tea."

"They are nice—once you can understand 'em,"
came from Orrie.

"Well, honey, that's all you need to remember
about most folks and you'll get along all right," he
told us.

"They'll have hogspudding, kiddley, and figgy
duff when we go down there again, Grandpa," said
Orrie. "If Columba's granfer spoke English, he'd
sure like you, too."

"Guess I'll stick with Cornelius," said Grandpa.
"I'm too old to be larnin' anything much new."

Wash never did give up all hope of finding Philip
Atterbury even if we did. He used to go out at night
and sit in front of our house and listen to the
coyotes out on the desert below the ledge. He swore
up and down one night there was a new sound in
one coyote's howl, a dog sound. "That there's Philip
Atterbury," he said. "I'd know his howlin' anywhere.

I sure heard it often enough. Sunday I'm going out after him."

He went, too. He even talked Orrie into going with him, but not me. I didn't like the desert. I wasn't scared of it—not if I kept in sight of our ledge and had lots of water, but it didn't seem very friendly to my way of thinking.

"Don't you kids go no farther than the old dry lake," Grandpa told them, "and you be back here by noontime." He gave Orrie his turnip watch and Wash a canteen of water.

They were back by noon all right. In fact, they were back by ten thirty and in, of all things, Mr. Stepney's buggy. All of us came out of our house to see it pull up. Mr. Stepney was in the front seat, Wash and Orrie in the back, their faces redder than beet slices and both bawling.

Mr. Stepney was a tall thin man with a long nose and a drooping dark mustache. "I brought your children back from the lake," he told Mama, tipping his hat.

"Hop down, kids," ordered Grandpa, after Mama thanked the mine owner politely.

Mr. Stepney looked almost embarrassed. "They

can't hop down, mam. They're going to have to be lifted down. They can't walk."

"Good Lord," said Grandpa Thompson. "What ails 'em?"

"Alkali poisoning. That's what. You better get the doctor up here."

Mama ran up to Orrie and lifted her down while Grandpa hoisted Wash up and out.

"Why'd you drink alkali water when you had good water from the reservoir with you?" demanded Grandpa.

"We didn't. We didn't," sobbed Orrie.

"Begging your pardon," broke in Belle Ann's father, "they didn't drink bad water. There isn't a drop out there to drink. They went across the lake walking barefoot. Lucky thing I was driving by. They'd been trailing a coyote. They never would have made it back here if I hadn't seen them."

I stared at Orrie's feet, which were sticking up in my face as Mama held her. They were bare, exactly as he said, and did they ever look terrible. They were bright red, swelled up half again their size and covered all over with water blisters. Wash's were just as bad.

Mama took one look, too, let out a little yelp, and said to me, "Callie, you go get the doctor up here right away."

I went. He was in his office where I hoped he'd be, and when he heard about the alkali poisoning he came running, too, alongside me, in spite of how hot it was. The doctor nodded to Mama, Grandpa, and Mr. Stepney, and then examined Wash's and Orrie's awful-looking feet. "Mrs. Perkins," he said to Mama, "the best thing you can do is keep these children's feet bandaged and keep them in bed. The one thing that'd help them Mojaveville, curse the luck, hasn't got."

"What's that?" Mama wanted to know.

"Cow dung—and the fresher the better!"

It sure got quiet now. Nobody knew what to say. Doctor Aubrey was blunter even than Miss Jennie-veva. I know I blushed. Grandpa looked like he wanted to laugh, and Mr. Stepney stared up at our ceiling.

"Where's the nearest cow?" asked Mama suddenly.

"Bass Ponds, mam," Mr. Stepney answered her.

Mama got her sunbonnet down from its peg, and said fiercely, "Mr. Stepney, will you take me to Bass Ponds right away?"

"Sure will," he told her.

Mama took up a bucket from behind the door, gave the doctor, Grandpa, and me one hard look, and out she and Mr. Stepney went. Dr. Aubrey sat down on a stool at our table. He put his hand over his face, so Grandpa and I couldn't see him laugh. All the same his shoulders were shaking. When he took down his hand, his mouth wasn't laughing, but his eyes were still crinkled up.

"Mr. Thompson, put the coffeepot on, please," he said to Grandpa. "We're in for a spell of waiting."

Grandpa went to the stove, and I went along with him to parch some more coffee beans while Wash and Orrie moaned, tossing on Mama's bed. "Do you think maybe we broke the ice with the Stepneys?" I asked him.

Grandpa was laughing, too. "Callie, honey, if this won't do it, I don't know what will."

It did, too. Mama and Mr. Stepney found the cow and got what the doctor had ordered. My sister and brother didn't like the treatment, but in a couple of days they were all right again except for sore feet.

The next Sunday Mama and Orrie and I went to Stepneys for tea. I thought we looked pretty good. Because we had water, which only cost $1.50 a month piped in now, we had white muslin summer dresses, too. They were just as white as Belle Ann's and just as starched. Mama looked really elegant in her dove gray silk dress with the black lace trim. I'd done her hair for her, and she'd put mine and Orrie's into curlpapers for ringlets. Grandpa said we were all his "pretty girls." Wash said Orrie and I looked "dumb," so I guessed we were really slickered up all right.

Mrs. Stepney's house was fancy—velvet-covered furniture and satin shining portieres and gold picture frames with pictures of dogs and horses and people in them. Their Chinese servant, who was Un Lung's nephew, brought in tea at four o'clock, little sandwiches and cookies and tea in a big silver pot. Orrie and I sat on a stiff-back sofa across from Belle Ann and talked about dolls, things we had given up years ago, while Mama talked about the school to Mrs. Stepney. I'd rather been at Trewhiddles' any day.

But Mama was pleased as punch. Nobody, not even Mr. Stepney, who had a cup of tea with us, opened his mouth once about that trip they'd made to Bass Ponds. When Mama had talked about how slow the school board was making plans for building a schoolhouse, Mr. Stepney offered her the Reba Mine right out. That was what Mama had been after all along, I guessed. Right out she accepted it. She knew she and Miss Jennieveva could swing the people on the city council around to the idea. Using the Reba wouldn't cost Mojaveville anything but a teacher's pay.

"Aren't the Stepneys nice folks, girls?" Mama asked, as we walked home that afternoon, all trying to crowd under Mama's parasol.

"Nope," Orrie said. "They ain't. They're comp'ny polite, that's all."

I agreed with Orrie, but didn't tell Mama that I did. And I hadn't liked it either when Mrs. Stepney asked if the Cousin Jacks were sending their children to our school. And I remembered, too, that they'd all left Mojaveville when people were dying with la grippe. Anyhow, one thing good had come out of our visit to Stepneys. We had a schoolhouse, even if it was a mighty peculiar one. What's more Orrie hadn't hit Belle Ann in the face. But, as I told myself, the Stepneys sort of owed something to Mojaveville—something more than a worked-out mine tunnel.

The school board met in the back room at Little Eva's the next night. Cornelius brought the cards and beer and listened in on what they said. He told Grandpa, who told us. The board decided they'd hire a lady, a maiden lady. She was going to get twenty dollars a month and room and board at Miss Jennieveva's, which was the most respectable place in town, even if there were a couple more hotels by now. The teacher had to stay a maiden lady, though. That was one of the rules. If she got married, she had to resign right away.

"Bring one in who's young," one of the school-board members had said to the others.

Mama nodded when she heard about this remark. "Yes, I like young teachers, too. They're stronger and recuperate faster from a day's work. The heat won't bother a young woman so much either."

Slum Gullion Slim brought in our teacher the next week. All of us kids and all of the men in town who weren't up in the mines came out to get a look at her. But none of us saw anything.

We were having a Santa Ana, a desert storm, the day she came. It started with a skinny cloud, a yellow one racing over the horizon from the east. Then the sand began coming toward us across the Mojave. We could stand on our ledge and watch it coming. Dust devils danced in front of it. They were columns of real hot air, with whirling creosote bushes they'd pulled up, roots and all, in the middle of them. Santa Anas were bad in parts of southern California that had crops planted in them. I couldn't see how it could hurt Mojaveville, though, unless it blew it away, the wood houses, that is. It'd take a real big wind to blow our old bottle house anywhere at all.

The Santa Ana hit the desert just before Miss McIntosh got up to Mojaveville. The desert dust wasn't pink like Mojaveville's. It was white. It had covered Slim Neuberger and his lady passenger all over as if they were covered with flour. Everybody knew Slim, of course, because he was expected, but as for her, she was sure a big mystery. She had a tarpaulin on over her dress and the veil on her hat was down over her face.

Slim pulled up to Miss Jennieveva's and called out "whoa" to his mules. We were right behind him, Gennys and Columba and Orrie and me. We saw the school board, all six of them, come forward at once to meet her, their hats in their hands to keep 'em from blowing away.

Then we saw Uncle Hiram shove one of them forward, saying. "Ace high! You say 'hello' to the schoolmarm for us, Nash." Mr. Nash was a bookkeeper at one of the mines, a short man with yellow hair.

Pink dust and tumbleweeds blowing all around him, Mr. Nash said, "Welcome to Mojaveville, Miss

McIntosh." Then he helped her down and took her inside Miss Jennieveva's.

We waited. Nobody came out, while the Santa Ana got worse, getting ready to blow us light kids off into the canyon. So we went home.

"Good thing we've got water piped in," I told Mama later. "We guess it'll take days to clean the teacher off."

"Mr. Nash, he's sure a polite man," Orrie said to her. "He went inside Miss Jennieveva's with the teacher, and he never came out. He was saying hello to her from the whole school board, but he couldn't see her and because she had a veil down, I don't think she could see him. It ain't much of a hello when nobody can see anybody else, is it, Mama?"

Mama said, "He never did come out, Callie?" She sounded thoughtful to me.

"Nope, we waited and waited. Neither of 'em did."

"Columba said Mr. Nash got first look at her," added Orrie.

Eph Miller got in some copybooks and McGuffey readers from San Burdoo right away, and a black-board, too. The third week in September we started to school a hundred feet inside the Reba.

It was the first time I ever had gone into a mine.

Ladies were supposed to be bad luck in one, worse than knockers, according to Gennys. But it was all right now. The Reba wasn't being worked.

It was sure a funny school. The sides, floor, and roof of the shaft were smooth gray rock. The teacher had a kerosene lamp on her desk, which was set up on one side of the shaft. Some of the rest of us had kerosene lamps set in front of us on stools so we could see to read by. Our chairs were in front of hers, all twelve of them, and the blackboard behind her. We didn't have desks yet. They were supposed to be coming from Los Angeles, a long ways away.

Miss Dorothea McIntosh, now that we finally got a look at her, was pretty. She had dark hair done up in a bun, and bangs in front of her face over her forehead, and she had nice, white skin. The first week she wore fancy dresses trimmed with beads and fringe. The second week, because of the heat, she switched to wearing calico, too, but she always wore a hat! She was a real lady.

It wasn't hard for her teaching us Perkinses or Belle Ann, particularly Belle Ann, who knew an awful lot of stuff we didn't. That was because her father was rich enough to buy books for her. Banjo and the Trewhiddles, Boscawens and Nanfans, they were harder to teach, though the Cornishmen were polite enough. Banjo hated school and let her know it, though he didn't call her "squaw," the way I guessed he wanted to. The Cornish kids had bad trouble with English, so bad Miss McIntosh put Gennys up close to her desk to tell her what they were saying. Then she moved me up close to tell her what Gennys was saying.

One day Columba told the teacher, when she didn't have her lesson done, that she guessed she had the *lurgies* the night before.

"What are they? Are they contagious?" I heard Miss Dorothea ask Gennys.

"No, she means she was lazy, mam," answered Gennys. "She did a wisht ole job of it, too. Columba, she'll do most things *clicky* if she can."

I knew at least what that all meant. "Miss Dorothea." I put up my hand and went to whisper in her ear, which smelled of Florida water. "Gennys says Columba, she'd done a bad job of her homework. She went at it sort of left-handed."

The teacher sighed. She sure did a lot of sighing in the old Reba mine during the days school was on. The rest of the time she spent riding around with Mr. Nash of the school board in his new rig, going down the ledge to Bass Ponds where it was cooler.

Miss Acheson thought he was "sweet" on her.

"How can you tell that, Miss Jennieveva?" I asked
her.

"Because he's such a awful pest," she snapped at
me. "He might as well live here instead of at the
Lion's Den."

I thought Miss Acheson was probably a little bit
jealous, but she was right about Mr. Nash because
around the middle of October Miss Dorothea told
folks she'd got engaged to him.

Mama wasn't very happy about this news.
"What'd she come up here for—to teach school or
catch herself a husband?" I heard her ask Grandpa.

"Well, honey," he told Mama, while he filled his
pipe, "ain't that what you did in marryin' Gideon.
You never even got around to teachin'. At least this
Miss McIntosh gave it a try."

Her try wasn't much of one, though. At Hal-
loween time she got married in a white dress to Mr.
Nash in Miss Jennieveva's parlor. I was there because I'd been working that morning and didn't go
home when I was supposed to. Neither did Orrie.
Un Lung had told us about the wedding coming
up.

We peeked through the portieres and saw the
preacher from Barstow make Miss Dorothea "Mrs.
Nash." We saw Miss Jennieveva, who was a witness,
all dolled up in a purple dress for a change, crying.

"That's because she ain't the bride," Orrie whis-pered to me.

Uncle Hiram stood up for Mr. Nash. He was really duded up in a pearl gray suit and dark gray derby. He looked clean. Orrie and I thought he looked better than the groom did, but he was still the same old Uncle Hiram.

When the short wedding ceremony was all over, Uncle Hiram kissed the bride on the cheek and yelled out, "One thing you can sure say about Mo-javeville, it's the happy hunting ground for old maids!"

Mrs. Nash, who wasn't our teacher anymore, laughed a little bit, but not much. Miss Jennieveva didn't even laugh. She gave the Duke a glare that would have blasted a rattler dead in midcrawl. I knew how she felt. I would have liked to bash in the Duke's head with a cuspidor, too.

Nobody caught Orrie and me peeking. Un Lung kept good watch for us and put his finger to his lips when we tiptoed out through the hallway back into the kitchen. Orrie and I were quiet as we walked home. Then she said, "Did you see it, too, Callie?"

"See what?"

"Miss Dorothea, she didn't have no veil and no flowers. That was too bad."

I nodded. Miller's didn't stock wedding veils yet,

and I didn't know of one white lace curtain in town. As for flowers, there weren't any at all in Mojave-ville, not even flowers for a wedding or to put on the graves in our cemetery.

Mama said she'd asked Slim a couple of times to bring her a rosebush from San Bernardino, but he kept forgetting it. It wasn't the sort of thing to stick in a man's mind, I guessed.

When we gave Mama the news about the wedding, she looked up from her sewing, and said, "There will have to be a new teacher then. I hope it doesn't take the school board all November to get one."

7 * The Gully

It didn't. Two weeks after Miss Dorothea moved
into a house Pa helped build for her and Mr. Nash,
Essie Jerome came. She was a little lady with curly
yellowish hair, big greenish blue eyes, and a funny
giggle. She wore calico and muslin dresses right
from the start, which made Orrie and me guess she
knew the Mojave and was from someplace around.
We were right. She hailed from San Burdoo and had

153

quit teaching for a while, but when she heard we
needed a teacher she came out to Mojaveville to
help out. We figured she thought she was rescuing
us. That's what Mama and Miss Jennieveva figured,
too, but we were wrong.

Mr. Adams, who was another one of the school
board, started to squire her right off. He was the
first one to meet her, just the way Mr. Nash was the
first one to meet Miss Dorothea. Miss Essie came in
by stagecoach, which traveled twice a week now
from Burdoo to our camp. Mr. Adams was a little
man, but it was easy for him to lift her down out of
the coach all the same, as if she didn't weigh a
thing. Orrie and I saw her turn pink.

Uncle Hiram wasn't there that day. He was out
prospecting with Grandpa and Mr. Cornelius, but
other school board men were there. We saw Mr.
Nash slap Mr. Adams on the back and wink and tell
him, "There's the queen of diamonds for you, Ben,"
as Mr. Adams went up to the stagecoach, where
Miss Essie was poking her head out.

"What do you 'spose that meant?" Orrie asked
me. Orrie had a real bad curiosity itch.

"I dunno," I told her. Miss Essie didn't have any
diamonds on her at all that I could see, only a little
gold locket.

Well, Miss Jerome taught us for a couple of weeks, and then one night she ran off with Mr. Adams to Barstow and got married to him.

Miss Jennieveva hit the roof when she found out, and she was the first to know because Miss Essie lived with her, too, the way Miss Dorothea had. I guessed it was because she'd lost another boarder, but that wasn't really it. "Callie," she told me. "I'm beginning to get blood in my eye what with these two schoolmarms upping and getting married in two months' time. I think I begin to smell a rat."

"What kind of a rat, Miss Acheson?"

She shook her head. "Well, I don't want to tell you right now, dear. There are some things you're still too young and innocent to know, but I'm going to have a little chat with your mama real soon."

She did, too. I wasn't invited, but Mama stomped home from it madder'n any wet hen I ever saw in the rain. She shut down her sun parasol and took off her hat and slammed them both down on her bed. "That Hiram!" she burst out with. "That miserable wretched Hiram Perkins! He is the most impossible man."

Wash asked, "What's the Duke gone and done now?"

"Nothing that Jennieveva and I can put our fin-

gers onto yet, but we have our suspicions, Washington." I could tell Mama was mad all the way
through, because she called my brother by his
whole name. She turned to me now. "Callie, when
your father's off work tonight, you go tell him I
want to meet him in Miss Jennieveva's parlor at
seven thirty."

"Why there, Mama? You know Pa hates parlors."

"Because it's neutral ground."

I didn't think Miss Acheson's parlor was neutral
ground for any man, but I held back from saying so.
Anyhow, at seven o'clock, I went down to the Lion's
Den and asked the first man who came out to get Pa
outside. Pa came right off, all dirty in his carpenter's
clothes. I noticed he was growing a beard.

"Pa, Mama wants to see you." I told him where
and what time.

"What about?" He was suspicious.

"I don't know, but I think maybe about smelling
out rats."

My answer seemed to puzzle him. "There're lots
of pack rats up here, but they don't smell so bad."

"Not pack rats, Pa."

He sighed. "All right, Callie, I'll get cleaned up,
and then I'll come see what your ma wants."

Mama saw him all right. She came back even

madder than she set out, and this time she was boiling. She burst out to me with a shotgun blast explo-
sion. "That Gideon! He told me Jennieveva and I
were crazy!"

Then she sat down at the table and began to
bawl. I felt sorry for her, but didn't know what I
could do to make her feel better other than pouring
her a cup of coffee. After all, I didn't even know
what she and Pa had fought about, but whatever it
was it wasn't about his beard, I was sure.

A month later, December now, we got another
teacher, Miss Martha Fraser. Like Miss Dorothea,
she came from Los Angeles. Miss Martha was a tall
lady with a lot of soft-looking brown hair, a wide
smile, brown eyes, round as marbles, and nice ways
about her. She was lots of fun. Orrie and Gennys
and Columba and me, we admired her a lot. So did
the boys, for a wonder. Because the weather had
changed for the better—it got so cold our school
rain barrel got ice on it—life was easier. We could
go outside the mine now and play games. Miss
Martha played tag and sometimes even baseball
with us. She turned out to be an awfully good pitcher
for a teacher.

Miss Fraser had lots and lots of beaux, including

one from the school board. He was Mr. Metzger, who had been one of Miss Jennieveva's boarders until he took up cheroot smoking, then Miss Jennieveva drove him out to go live in the Lion's Den. Miss Martha didn't seem too serious about any of her beaux that Miss Acheson and Mama and I could see. When our third teacher went buggy riding with Mr. Metzger, Miss Jennieveva tried to keep watch on her and had me tell Mama if I'd seen them together, too. It wasn't too hard for Miss Acheson to do her spy work with Miss Martha living at her place.

About Christmastime Miss Fraser had some big news for us. A couple more Cornish families with kids had come up to Mojaveville, and that finally lit a fire under the school board. They decided to build a schoolhouse for us out on top of a ledge beyond the town.

"But the only way to get over there is to grab a bush and climb up the sides of the place," I said to her, after she told us.

"No, Callie," she explained. "They're going to build a bridge across the arroyo."

"Oh." I guessed that'd do the trick all right.

Then she went on to say, "To celebrate, children, we're not having any school the day before Christ-

mas vacation starts. We're going on a picnic instead!"

That suited all of us Perkinses just fine. What
with Mama working and us being a split-up family,
we hadn't been on a picnic since we left Sacramento.

"Where'll we have it?" I wanted to know. "Bass
Ponds?"

"No, out in a pretty little canyon in the desert I
know. It'll be nice this time of the year."

"You been buggy ridin' out there with somebody?" asked Wash, bold as brass.

Miss Fraser blushed, so we knew she had.

Mama bought a chicken from Miss Jennieveva.
Grandpa, who was home for a few days resting from
prospecting and Mr. Cornelius's cooking, killed it.
Then Mama fried it for us in bacon fat and flour. It
sure looked good and smelled good, too, when we
put it in our basket to take to the picnic. Orrie and I
had decided we'd share it with Gennys and Columba if they'd share their Cornish pasties, the kind
without turnips in them, with us. Orrie purely hated
turnips.

Miss Martha called for us at eight o'clock in the
morning in a mud wagon. She could drive a team of

mules as well as any man in Mojaveville. The twelve
of us who were going rode inside the wagon down
the ledge and out into the desert, singing "Beulah
Land" and other songs. It was a nice day even if the
sun was shining. We had our jackets on because it
was pretty chilly that early, but by noontime we
were running races in our shirts and dresses. We
kept our shoes on, though. Our Perkins alkali poisoning had taught us and every other kid in camp, too,
not to go barefoot on the desert.

We had a lot of games and then ate our lunch,
and afterward Miss Martha told us, if we'd be extra
careful of rattlesnakes, we could split up sides and
choose partners and go out prospecting, a thing
some of the boys wanted to do.

Wash and the Nanfan boys had brought funny-
looking little hammers and ore sample bags with
them. Gennys and Columba groaned when they saw
them and even Belle Ann looked down at the mouth.
Because they had the prospecting tools, the boys
got to do the choosing up. Wash chose Belle Ann,
because he was still sweet on her and here was his
chance to show off. Then he chose Banjo because he
was his best friend and then, darn his hide, me.
Orrie, she went with Gennys and Columba and the
biggest Nanfan boy, Jenkin. The rest of the kids and

Miss Martha went with his brother, Hodge. I'd rather have gone with one of the Nanfans, but it wouldn't do me any good to bellyache to Miss Martha. Once somebody chose sides in her school, a kid really got "chose." She laughed when Hodge told her that he and she'd "strike it rich" that day. Then she told us all to be back at the mud wagon by three o'clock. It was one thirty then.

Belle Ann was duded up that day something fierce in a pale blue ruffly dress with a dark blue sash. To keep the sun off her face, so it wouldn't get brown, she didn't have a calico sunbonnet like the rest of us. Hers was made out of white straw and had blue plaid ribbons. Miss Jennieveva had told me something about Belle Ann and why she was the way she was. She'd been raised part of her life by her grandmother who lived on Nob Hill in San Francisco and was a rich old lady. She sent her clothes from there, and she was responsible for Belle Ann's having private teachers for a while and for the funny way she talked. That day I thought Belle Ann looked awful. And it was awful the way she stared at Wash out from under her eyelashes when he showed off in front of her, walking on his hands. I almost wished he'd get alkali poisoning on them.

Miss Martha's canyon, about three miles from Mojaveville, was just as pretty as she said it was. It was full of big yellow-white yucca plants, which I thought were the nicest in the whole desert. They looked like a whole forest of giant Christmas-tree candles to me. Wash and the rest of us prospected it first after the others had gone, all of us standing around while he hit this rock and that rock with the hammer, hunting for silver.

It didn't take Wash long to hit nearly every rock he could reach while Banjo lugged the empty ore sack and stood over him, waiting. Then they both decided we'd try another place where we'd maybe have better luck. There was a gully Wash had seen from the buckboard that morning on the way. "There's horn silver in that old gulch," he told us, "and we can get there and back easy by three. You be our timekeeper, Callie." And he gave me Grandpa Thompson's turnip watch out of his pocket.

I knew now why Wash had chosen me to go along with him. It was because I could tell time! He and Banjo couldn't yet, and I knew Belle Ann wasn't so good at it either unless both hands were right at the hour. With Roman numerals they couldn't do it at all, any one of them, and that was what Grandpa's old watch had, all right. I sighed and put it in my pocket, then tied my bonnet strings again and tramped out of the canyon behind my brother and the other two, expecting to have a horrible time.

I did, too, just standing around and telling him every fifteen minutes what time it was, feeling like a cuckoo clock. I hoped he'd head back pretty soon, but he wouldn't. I was getting boreder and boreder, standing breathing down his neck while he and Banjo banged old rocks, and Belle Ann counted sand lizards out loud as they ran across the bottom of the gully we were in.

At two o'clock when Belle Ann was up to twelve, Banjo looked at the sky, then up at the mountains way behind the narrow, steep, open-at-both-ends gulch we were prospecting in. The sky was dark gray-black up there. While I stood staring in the direction he looked, I saw some lightning flick across it.

"There's a storm up there," I said to Belle Ann. I talked to her about the weather.

"Yes," she told me, "but there isn't any storm down here, California. It's a lovely day."

Banjo gave the both of us a look that almost said "dumb squaws" right out loud. Then he went over to Wash and squatted down next to him. I thought Banjo was acting a little bit funny. He kept staring over his shoulder, and when my brother told him to put an ore lump in the sample sack, he didn't. He stood up, stared at the mountains, then shrugged his shoulders and went back to helping Wash prospect.

"What time is it, Callie?" Belle Ann asked me, yawning, a little while after Banjo had stood up and she'd spotted her seventeenth lizard.

I hauled out Grandpa's watch. "Near on to two forty-five." I was about to add, "Time to go back," but then I heard it—the strange sound. "Hey, listen." I said instead. "I hear something! Stop hammering, Wash!"

He wouldn't. Instead he yelled over his shoulder at me. "You just think you hear a rattler, Callie. Well, you don't. Because of my hammering, there ain't a snake around here for ten miles."

"It ain't a snake. I know what they sound like, too," I yelled back, truthfully, because Hodge had killed one up behind the Reba one day. "Now, Wash, you shut up and listen!"

Because I was the oldest even if I was a "squaw," everybody did shut up and listen to what I'd heard. It was a roaring sound, dull and far away, but coming nearer, too.

Banjo's eyes got big as bottle bottoms. "Run!" he screamed out. "Run 'fore it gits to us!"

"What? What?" hollered Wash.

"Run! Run for yer life!"

We did run, in all directions out of the gulch and back into it, and then I noticed that Banjo wasn't really running at all. He was climbing up the side of it, hauling himself all the way up by rocks and bushes as fast as he could.

"He means *up!*" I yelled at Wash and Belle Ann. I figured what a Mojave Indian did in the desert, we better do, too. They heard me. Where they were, Wash deeper inside the gulch and Belle Ann at its opening, they started to climb. I was halfway between Belle Ann and Banjo and going up as fast as I could manage, slipping and sliding on the crumbly rocks.

I was just about all the way to the top when it happened. The flash flood came. It came with a terrible roaring down the gully we were in, bringing whole trees and mesquite bushes and everything else that had been in its path with it. From where I was, it looked like a whole mile high of solid, racing dark brown water.

I hollered out, "Wash! Wash!" scared because he was closest to where it was coming down from. I was up high enough to be out of its way, but I kept on clawing at the rocks a little farther up. The top

was where I wanted to be. In a few minutes I
hauled myself over the rim of the gulch onto a place
about twenty feet across and fell flat on my face
down on the rocks. My heart was beating so fast I
thought it would jump out of me. Belle Ann, who
had dirt and blood all over her face where she'd
scraped it climbing, wasn't far away from me, on
her hands and knees, bending over staring down
into the gully as if she never had seen water before.
I looked for Banjo and saw him running back along
the top of the ledge fast as he could.

Like me he was yelling, "Wash! Wash!"

I got up and ran behind him, catching up with
him just in time to help grab my brother by the hair
of his head and drag him up where it was safe. The
brown water was up to Wash's waist, but he was
hanging on to a tough bush with good roots. If the
flood had caught him any deeper, it would have carried him downstream and either drowned him or
bashed him to death against the rocks in its way.

Wash was whiter than a sheet as he got up shaking, and stood with Banjo and me while the flash
flood poured out of the gully. Soon it was all over.
The water was gone, roaring away out onto the
Mojave. All that was left of it in a few minutes was
mud and a couple of carried-down tree branches.

Wash's hammer and the ore sack weren't anywhere to be seen. Neither was the little prickly pear bush I'd been standing by when I first heard that awful roaring noise.

"Gosh," came from Wash. "What was that?"

"That was a Mojave desert flood," Banjo answered him.

"But where'd all that water come from?" I asked him. "There must'a been fifteen feet of it, Banjo."

"There was a rainstorm up in the mountains, Callie."

"All *that* water from a rainstorm maybe miles and miles up north of us?"

He nodded. "Sure. It's so dry out here the rain don't sink in the ground."

I guessed I knew what he meant even if it was hard to believe that such a thing could happen.

"What'll we do now?" asked Wash, looking at Banjo. The Mojave Indian, not Wash, was our leader now.

But before Banjo could answer him, we heard a yelp from Belle Ann. She was standing up now, too, and was pointing down at something we couldn't see toward the narrowest end of our ledge.

We ran up to her. Then we saw it—a rattlesnake, a great big thick one. It wasn't coiled to strike. It was just lying there limp, and it was wet, not dusty dry the way rattlers usually are. The narrow end of the ledge sloped down lower than the part we were on. The flood had washed up onto it. That was where the snake had come from, out of the flood water.

My brother picked up a big rock. But all of a sudden Belle Ann grabbed his arm. "No, Washington," she cried out. "Don't kill it. It's been hurt. Leave it alone."

My brother didn't need a lot of convincing to leave it be. He put down the rock carefully and we all backed away as far as we could get, all except Banjo. He didn't go near the rattler, but he looked at it good, then he came back to us. "He won't be hurtin' nobody for a long time—not now," he said to us. "If a pack rat came up here to get away from the flood, it'd be safe with him. He's been washed out'a his hole somewhere up the gully. All we got to do is leave him alone."

"Like animals in a forest fire?" asked Wash.

"Yes, probably just like that," answered Belle Ann. She was a real sight. Her dress was all ripped and her straw hat gone, but she didn't seem to care any more than I did how she looked. Maybe she didn't care so much about clothes after all.

"That was real nice of you, not to let Wash kill that poor sick old snake," I said to her.

"I'm not the monster you think I am, California, you and Gennys and your sister and the others," was her answer. And then she did a very exciting thing, another thing that made me like her for all that she was so different from the rest of us. The flood had left a place in the side of our gulch that was solid mud, with no rocks in it at all, for twenty feet down. Belle Ann sat down with her legs dangling over the edge, gave herself a push with her hands, and down she slid in the mud, all the way to the bottom.

"She likes being dirty," said Wash, admiring her more than ever.

Because Belle Ann had showed us the easiest way down and because we were all a mess anyhow, we did what she did and left the ledge to the half-dead rattler. When I got to the bottom I thought of something. Orrie!

"Orrie and the others," I yelled out. "Where're they? Where's Miss Martha?" I turned to Banjo. "Banjo, they didn't have a real, live smart Mojave Indian to help them out the way we did!"

He shook his head, agreeing with me.

Half a mile out in the desert we found Miss

Martha, Hodge Nanfan, and the other two. They'd
been lucky, real lucky. Since there had been three
ladies to one man in their group, they made Hodge
give up prospecting and go out of the gullies with
them to hunt for a cactus in bloom, something a lot
more interesting to them than rocks. They saw the
flood all right, saw it come gushing brown out of a
whole flock of gullies and run right into the desert
and sink into the sand. They'd been scared, too, and
had run up on a little rise when they saw it coming,
but it hadn't got anywhere at all near them. We saw
the wet brown-covered sand where it had disappeared. That was all there was now of that fifteen
feet of water that had nearly drowned the four of
us.

When Miss Fraser saw us coming toward her, she
let out a scream of pleasure, hiked up her skirts to
her knees, and came flying toward us, crying. She
didn't give a hoot about the mud that was all over
us. She hugged us, all four of us at the same time,
and kissed us. "I thought you were dead!" she
bawled. "The mud wagon's wrecked and the mules
are dead!" When she got her breath, she told us,
"We saw what was left of the wagon, nothing but
boards, and the body of one of the mules is over
there."

"The mule, he got smashed on the rocks," Hodge added. "I looked at him good." Hodge's freckles stood out plain like bright copper cents, his face was so pale.

"Where's Orrie? Where's my sister?" I asked. I cared about the poor old mules, but I cared a lot more about her.

"And Jenkin and Columba and Gennys?" came from Belle Ann.

Miss Martha shook her head. "I don't know, children. I don't know. We haven't seen them."

Now I started to cry, too. I flung my arm out in the direction of the gully we'd got out of. "They're still back there someplace?"

Miss Martha got down on her knees and held me close to her. "Callie, oh, Callie, they must be. The Mojave's flat as a pancake around here except for the rise we were on. There isn't a living thing in sight for miles except for us."

What she said was true. There wasn't anybody out there on the desert but our teacher and us kids and the dead mules. Now Belle Ann was crying, too, and so were the two Cornish girls, smaller kids than we were.

Not Wash. "If we got out alive, maybe they did, too," he said to Miss Fraser.

Banjo put in, "The flood's over. Why don't we go back and look for Orrie and the others, mam?"

"But where would we start?"

"In the canyon where we had our picnic. We could start yelling for them when we get there." Wash was thinking.

Miss Martha wiped her eyes with her skirt. "It's as good a place as anywhere else."

Then she got up. "Well, come along, children. We'll try to find them. You stay together this time. Keep close to me. Banjo, you know this country. You lead the way."

Even if I was bawling and plenty scared for Orrie, I still noticed how proud Banjo was of being leader again. I figured Miss Martha wouldn't ever have any more trouble with him in school and neither would I. He thought we were good squaws now.

So we started walking back toward the gullies and canyons beneath the mountains. The picnic canyon was a mess, just like the one we had been trapped in. One of our mud wagon's wheels was in it, standing up just the way it should, but with no wagon around it. Other canyons and gullies branched off from it. Some of them had sticky mud and piled-up bushes in them, too. Others were completely dry.

I didn't understand why some were dry and some wet. "What'd the flood do?" I asked Banjo. "Did it only come down some of the gullies?"

"That's right, Callie, the ones that branched off the right way for the flood to go. Maybe some of the others didn't branch right. Maybe others were dead-end gulches, the kind that's only open at the front end."

I took a deep breath. "I think maybe we better look in the open-ended muddy ones first, don't you, Miss Martha?"

Miss Fraser touched my arm. "That would be wisest, Callie, I think."

I was surprised when Belle Ann came over to me and put her arm around my shoulder. "You remember, California," she told me, "we got trapped and we got out, didn't we? I'm going to be right beside you and Washington, remember?"

"You're a good friend, Belle Ann." I never thought I'd say that to her, but she came through in a pinch and she was brave! I almost forgave the Stepneys for running out when la grippe came.

We tromped through the drying mud, which caked our shoe tops, yelling and calling, yelling and calling. Nobody answered us in any of the flooded gullies we went into. A couple of them were so choked with stuff the water had carried down that nobody could get through it or climb over it—not even Wash or Banjo or Hodge. Those places we stood outside and hollered into.

I was still crying. So were Belle Ann and the Cornish girls, a little. It was hard for me to call, but Wash and Banjo and Miss Fraser still had the lung power. Finally our teacher came over to me and the other girls and said, "It's no use, Callie. We're going to have to walk back to Mojaveville and get help. Men will have to haul all the debris away in the blocked gulches and search for. . . ."

I knew what awful thing she meant, and it made me shiver and cry harder. She thought the others were dead.

Banjo heard Miss Martha. "No mam," he told her. "I know this part of the Mojave. There are three dead-end gulches we ain't tried yet. We got to try 'em all."

We followed Banjo as he struck off east. One dead-end gully was wide, shallow, and dry. It didn't have anything in it at all except prickly pear and jack-rabbits that ran away when we came inside, yelling. By the time we walked around to the second one I was pretty tired out.

We found them in the second gully, a narrow,

long deep one, so dark it was like night inside it. By now we were all too hoarse to yell anymore. They were three quarters of the way inside it, sitting on some rocks in a shaft of sunshine, all four of them, Orrie, Jenkin, Columba, and Gennys, right as rain.

Their mouths fell open when they saw us, slopped up with mud and four of us with our clothes torn.

"Callie," Orrie cried out to me, "what's happened to you? You got dirty brown mud all over you!"

I couldn't explain it to her. Belle Ann had to do that while I sat on another rock and cried. "It was a flood. We got caught in it."

"What flood?" asked Jenkin Nanfan.

"The flash flood that come down out'a the mountains," Banjo explained to him.

Gennys shook her head. "We didn't know nothing about any flood, Banjo. That'd be auld woman's *widdle*, wudden it?"

"Well, there certainly was a flood, a terrible one, Gennys," Miss Martha told her.

"Didn't you hear anything at all, Oregon, a sort of roaring noise?" demanded Belle Ann.

"No, we heard a little rumbling, I guess, but we thought maybe it was thunder in the mountains," said Orrie, shaking her head.

Her answer stopped me crying. "Well, you were

lucky, all of you, not to have been caught in it." I
was almost mad at Orrie now that we'd found her.
Here she was clean, safe and sound, and not worried
like Wash and me. I pulled Grandpa's watch out of
my pocket and read the time off to her. "It's past five
o'clock. You ought'a been out of here a long time
ago."

"I busted my pa's watch. It fell out 'a my pocket
on a rock," said Jenkin.

"You dumb—" I was about to say "Cousin Jack"
when Miss Martha stopped me.

"Children, we have to start back to Mojaveville at
once!"

So back we went across the desert. It was a good
thing it was December, which was coolish toward
sunset, or we never would have made it. Almost all
our water was gone. I'd lost my canteen, which was
the only one in our prospecting party, when I
climbed up the rocks. The flood took it when it
slipped off over my shoulder. Hodge and Jenkin
shared theirs, but by dark when the buckboards
coming from town found us a mile from home, that
was gone, too. Walking across the sand was thirsty
work.

We saw their lanterns coming across the flats and
because we had four good yellers left among us,

Jenkin and his prospectors, they told our rescuers which way to come. Pa, Uncle Hiram, Mr. Metzger, and Mr. Stepney were there with some other men, Cornishmen. They all had shotguns and pistols with them and hard looks on their faces. Pa was the first one to call out, "Where the hell you kids been so long?"

"In a flash flood, Pa!" Orrie yelled back, recogniz-ing his voice. "Callie and Wash, they nearly got drowned. There was a rattlesnake with 'em, too."

Then Pa jumped down and grabbed the three of us and hugged us. He wasn't mad anymore. "Your ma sent me. She's half crazy with worry. You should 'a been home hours ago."

Under his elbow I saw Belle Ann crying against her father's coat and saw Mr. Metzger get down out of a buckboard, too. Miss Martha ran to him, and he put his arms around her and patted her on the back while she began to bawl some more. Then he kissed her on the forehead. She smiled up at him and stopped crying. I guessed I knew what that meant.

Another schoolteacher had bit the dust!

Uncle Hiram knew it, too. I saw him grinning up on the buckboard seat, and then he made an O shape with his fingers. Columba guessed too what was going on with our teacher. She didn't run to her pa the way Gennys did. She just sat down on a desert rock and said to me, when I got ready to get into the mud wagon with Pa, "My dear *sawl,* even if it wodden bad fer us, I'm *rumped* up like a *winnard.*"

I didn't begin to know what she meant. The words were all new to me, but the way she spoke made me think that I probably felt the same, too.

8 ✳ Miss Nellie

"*Rumped* up like a *winnard*," I learned a couple of days later, only meant "cold and hungry"—not down at the mouth at all.

Mama cried and cried when she heard about our narrow escape, then she wiped her eyes and cooked us all a pancake supper—at eleven o'clock at night. Uncle Hiram and Pa had come in to eat it with us. Having everybody together again was real nice.

Then at midnight, when I was just starting to yawn because the day had been so exciting, they'd gone back to the Lion's Den.

"Gid, he's still holdin' out, honey," I heard Grandpa tell Mama after Pa'd left.

"Yes," she'd said to him, and that was all she said.

Pa came up Christmas Eve and Christmas morning to be with us and brought us some horehound and peppermint candy. Uncle Hiram brought us three oranges apiece. They were full of seeds, but were still good. Miss Jennieveva gave us twenty-five cents each extra on our Saturday wages. I never knew what Wash did with his, but Orrie and I spent ours on hair ribbons. Mama gave Wash a new shirt she'd sewed for him, and Orrie and me new calico dresses, dark blue ones with red and white rickrack on the sleeves. For her we had a fancy present, a real live rosebush, one that Slim Neuberger said would have pink roses on it. She planted it in front of our door and watered it morning and night.

But Mojaveville was too much for a San Bernardino rose. In January it shriveled up and died when a Santa Ana blew down on us.

That was the week before our new teacher came. She was a Miss Nellie Remington. Miss

Martha had married Mr. Metzger three days after Christmas.

Miss Nellie was black haired and had big teeth and little gray eyes and was tall and skinny. Her voice was very high pitched. "She's almost as homely as Miss Jennieveva, but not quite. Nobody could be that homely," Orrie whispered to me that first day in Miss Remington's class.

Well, Miss Nellie moved in with Miss Acheson, too, in the same room Miss Dorothea, Miss Essie, and Miss Martha had. I cleaned it on Saturdays, so I knew a lot about the teachers and who used Florida Water and who used Orange Flower Water and who used Florestan Eau de Cologne. Miss Nellie didn't use anything to make her smell sweet unless it was vanilla out of the kitchen. I told Mama about how homely she was and that she didn't have more than five dresses and no toilet water.

"I think maybe she won't get married on us," I told her.

Mama was trying to make some bread that had got stale fresh again by soaking it in milk and water and then baking it once more in a hot oven. I was turning over the pickled beef in the big crock, a thing I'd been doing for nine days. Tomorrow we'd be able to cook it. She sighed and asked me, "Callie, how many bachelors are there here in Mohave-ville?"

"Hundreds, I guess."

"And how many on the school board?"

I thought for a minute. "Two left—Uncle Hiram and old Mr. Wilcox. That's all that's left."

Mama put the bread in the oven and shut the door before she asked another question. "Has it ever occurred to you that all three teachers who've come up here have married school-board members?"

"Well, sure it did, Mama. They were just about the first men each time to lay eyes on the teachers."

"Indeed, they were." She straightened up and wiped her hands on her apron. "Now I grant you it was their duty to greet a new teacher, but why *one at a time?*"

"I don't know, Mama."

"Jennieveva and I think it was all arranged and by your uncle Hiram at that!"

"But what'd the Duke do?"

"We think he's behind the whole thing, putting ideas in the men's heads and running a matrimony bureau."

"Uncle Hiram! He likes old bachelors."

"He likes playing games with people better than that, Callie."

I thought for a long, long minute about what Mama and Miss Acheson suspicioned. Then I remembered what the Duke had said to Mr. Nash when Miss McIntosh came. It was, "ace high." When Miss Essie arrived, Mr. Nash had said something about a "queen of diamonds" to Mr. Adams and slapped him on the back. I remembered, too, what Mr. Cornelius had told Grandpa—that he'd brought in cards with the beer when the school board met the very first time in the back room of Little Eva's saloon.

"Mama," I announced so loud she nearly dropped the lid she was going to put back on the pickling crock. "I think I got something to tell you."

So I told her about the two and two I'd put together and the four I'd got and did she blaze up. "They drew *cards! Cards*—to see who'd court the teachers as they came up here?"

"Yes, and old Mr. Wilcox must'a drawn the low card and got Miss Remington."

Mama practically ripped off her apron. Then she grabbed down her blue shawl and mine from pegs on the door, took a hold of my hand and pulled.

"Where we going, Mama?" I called out to her, as she dragged me outside. She sure didn't care about that stale bread of ours.

"To Jennieveva Acheson's. You tell her what you just told me, Callie."

I did, too.

Miss Jennieveva swelled up like a poisoned frog. Her eyes popped out of her head while her face turned redder and redder. Then she exploded. "It's the doings of Hiram Perkins, Hope. Nobody else. The rest of 'em on the school board don't have minds that think that sneakin' way. And his plot's working again, too."

"What do you mean?" snapped Mama.

"Even if he's older'n the hills, that skinflint, Mr. Wilcox, that foxy grandpa, has taken notions to himself lately. He bought a buggy. You and I know he wouldn't spend money for nothing he didn't intend to get some good use out of. Tonight he's taking Miss Remington out riding with him."

"Can't you stop them, Jennieveva?"

Miss Acheson shook her head. "Not any way I can think of less than shooting Mr. Wilcox or his horse. She's probably a goner, too. Nobody else has come courtin' her, and she told me she wants to get married." Miss Jennieveva sniffled when she spoke. I felt sorry for her. She wiped her eyes on a lacy-looking handkerchief. "There's no help for it, I guess. The children up here'll never get educated. The school board cares more about brides than book learning."

Mama spoke up fiercely. "Yes, there is a way, Jennieveva. Don't you cry. We're going to get Hiram off the school board!"

"And get another *bachelor* on it?"

"No," Mama sounded fiercer than ever. "We're going to put *you* on it in his place."

I was so surprised that on the way back home with Mama, before I could stop my mouth, I said, "The Duke isn't so bad he has to be kicked off the school board, is he? He was nice to me when la grippe was here, and he helped sober the doctor up and he didn't really mean anything bad when he sent me that chuckawalla."

Mama was biting her lips. "Your uncle Hiram's got a misplaced funny bone." She glared at me almost as if she was mad at me, too. "When we were up in Idaho Territory, he did a terrible thing."

"What was that?" I figured he'd robbed or shot somebody.

"He answered an ad in a Portland, Oregon, newspaper he got hold of."

"Lots 'a people answer ads, don't they?"

Mama was stepping along fast. I practically had to run to keep up with her. "They don't claim to be handsome young ladies!"

"Uncle Hiram?"

She nodded. "That's what he did. A young man from Portland said in his ad that he was too busy working, making money, to meet eligible young ladies and that he was lonesome. He asked 'interested ladies' to write him. Hiram did."

"That's terrible!"

"It gets worse," she told me. "Hiram won a daguerreotype of a pretty girl in a poker game, and he sent it to Portland. The young man naturally sent his picture back. Letters kept going and coming so fast between them that it made me dizzy to hear about them—love letters, mind you. Finally this man came all the way up into Idaho to meet this girl."

"But he couldn't ever find her, Mama!"

"Of course not. She wasn't there at all. She lived in Massachusetts, and had been the sweetheart of the miner who put up her picture in the poker game. By the time Hiram sent the picture the miner'd gone back there himself. The man from Portland hunted over half of Idaho Territory before he knew he'd been tricked. It cost him a pretty penny traveling around, too, before someone told him Hiram had been doing the writing. When he heard this, he came gunning for your precious

uncle. Hiram skedaddled out of Idaho one step
ahead of a cocked forty-four." She stopped before
our door and gave me a sour look. "Now, let me hear
you defend the Duke of Kansas. He's a meddler in
other folks' lives!"

I had to agree. That was an awful trick he pulled
on the man from Portland, and he hadn't been honest either about the schoolteachers and the school
board. "He's a mean meddler!"

"Callie, the school board anywhere is a place of
responsibility," she told me. "It has no room on it for
men of Hiram Perkins's stripe. We'll have to get him
off it somehow."

"How, Mama?"

She pushed open the door, not caring a bit that
our house was full of black smoke coming out of the
oven because our baked-over bread was burning up.
"I'll think of something. I don't know what just yet,
Callie, but something will come to me. You all are
going to get educated yet."

For a couple of weeks things were peaceful in
Mojaveville. Mr. Wilcox was too old to be a fast
courter, so we had Miss Nellie teaching us all the
way through February and March. She kept company all that time with him, though, and folks sort

of guessed she wouldn't last out the year either. They were busy taking bets on it, Mama heard in Miller's store.

April Fool's Day in Mojaveville was exciting. The men in the camp shot up a dummy in the middle of the street with pistols. I think they thought it was fun, but like Gennys said it left one "weak as a robin" seeing it twitch around when bullets hit it— even if it was a game. I was glad Pa and Grandpa didn't do it. They weren't even there to watch Uncle Hiram and the other menfolks.

Pa came up to our house a couple of times for dinner that month. One night, a night he wasn't invited, he showed up dragging something along with him, our dog, Philip Atterbury. We heard them coming before we saw them. All the way up to our slope Philip Atterbury howled and dug in his claws as if he wasn't very glad to be back home.

After Pa tied him to the table leg, we all started at once to ask him where he'd found him.

Pa held up his hands for us to keep quiet, then explained. "Down in Mica Gulch, there's a mine where I been carpentering called the Sequoia, a big one with lots of men workin' it. That's where this mutt's been living all the time."

"He wasn't out with the coyotes at all?" Wash sounded disappointed.

Pa was plain disgusted. "Take a look at him. Are his ribs showin'?"

They weren't. Philip Atterbury looked as if he was in the pink of condition. He sure didn't seem to have missed us at all. When we tried to pet him, he ducked away at the end of his rope even worse than he used to.

"Well, what'll we do with this tramp mutt?" asked Pa of the three of us. "He's a no-good dog, always was and always will be."

I didn't care much one way or the other. Neither did Orrie. But Wash did. "He's our dog all the same."

"He'll run back to the Sequoia first chance he gets," warned Pa.

"Then I'll go out to Mica Gulch and get him back!"

Pa gave us three a hug, and a handshake to Grandpa and off he went, but not before he told Wash. "Well, son, if you're dead set on keepin' this dog, you've got your work cut out for you."

When he was gone, I asked Mama privately. "Why didn't you tell Pa about getting Uncle Hiram off the school board?"

"He wouldn't listen to me, that's why. Remember I did try to suggest to him that Hiram was up to no good some time ago." She was getting ready to make biscuits and had flour all over her hands. "This job has to be done some other way, Callie." Mama smiled to herself. "And I begin to see how at last."

The next day Philip Atterbury got away again, and off he ran to Mica Gulch, five miles away. Wash went after him and brought him back and tied him up. Two days afterward he got loose again, and back he went to the Sequoia mine.

"What's so good about Mica Gulch, Wash?" asked Orrie.

"There's thirty men there feedin' him and makin' over our fool dog," answered our brother, hauling Philip Atterbury over our threshold for the fourth time. Then when he got him inside, he added, panting the same way the dog did, "How can the three of us keep up with thirty men?"

"I don't want to try," Orrie told him. I agreed with her.

Five and six times Wash went after Philip Atterbury. By this time they were both pretty tuckered out. Everybody was disgusted—even Banjo who'd gone along on trips three and four.

"Wash, dear, why don't you give up?" Mama asked him one night after the dog had got away again, leaping past my brother before he could even get him tied to the table leg.

"Nope," said Wash. "I won't have folks sayin' I'm a quitter."

"Neither will Philip Atterbury," put in Orrie.

I admired my brother's stubbornness when for the eighth time he brought Philip Atterbury home. This time right into Miller's store to show Mama he wasn't about to give up. I was there buying some tatting thread for Miss Jennieveva.

"You're sure wearing out shoe leather, boy," Mr. Miller said to Wash. "How many times you been after that mutt by now?"

"Eight times."

Mr. Miller shook his head. "That's a determined animal you got there. All that energy you and he are puttin' in is going to waste."

"What do you mean?" asked Wash.

"I mean I think I ought to put you and that dog of yours to work."

"Philip Atterbury work? Doing what?" I couldn't help but ask, even if it wasn't any of my business.

"Well, Callie," said Mr. Miller, "as you know, I'm the postmaster here in Mojaveville. If that dog always heads for the same place the way folks say he does, I don't see any reason why he can't carry the mail there, do you?"

My mouth must have fallen open. "Huh?"

"Sure. Wash will go fetch the dog back up here to me twice a week. I'll sew up little saddlebags for this mutt, and he can take the Sequoia folks' mail to them. He'll be able to carry a lot more than Wash could himself. I'll pay you ten cents a week, Wash. It'll be cheaper than sending it by mule team. That mine's way off the beaten track. How about it, boy?"

Wash was so astonished he could only nod and nod. Finally, though, he found his voice. "What'll you pay Philip Atterbury?"

Mr. Miller didn't smile at bit. "All he can eat in biscuits at this end of his route."

Wash was quiet for a minute. "The ten cents is all right with me," he told the storekeeper, "but I'll wear out lots 'a shoes if I'm gonna' keep this up. So how about ten cents and shoe leather?"

Mr. Miller laughed. "Done!"

Wash stuck out his hand, shook Mr. Miller's, and handed over Philip Atterbury's rope to him.

I got to know what Mama had in mind the week Wyatt Earp came up to Mojaveville. I was a lot more interested in her secret planning than in Mr. Earp, but all the same I paid him some heed. He was handsome for a gunfighter, I thought. He was tall and had light blue eyes and brown hair. His suit was a plain pepper-and-salt gray one, and he didn't

even carry a gun that I could see, though Banjo said
he had a Buntline Special in his coat pocket all
right. Mr. Earp didn't talk much; too, he had a hard
way of setting his jaw. Those were the only things
that made him seem like a marshal to me. I couldn't
see what was supposed to make kids so crazy about
him at first, but then he hauled out a handful of
nickels for candy at Miller's. I guessed maybe that
he liked kids so much because he was single. After a
while I got to like him, too, while we trailed around
Mojaveville after him. I even shushed up my
brother when he wanted to ask him all about the
Clanton outlaws and the terrible gunfight at the
horse corral in Tombstone, Arizona Territory, two
years back. I figured Mr. Earp didn't want to talk
about it much, and I was right. Mr. Cornelius told
Grandpa that not a single word about it could be
pried out of the marshal by anybody.

"Well, what did you think of the wonderful Mr.
Earp?" Mama asked me the night he went back to
San Bernardino. She'd waited on him in Miller's
when he bought a pair of sleeve garters.

"He was nice, Mama, but I'd rather know what
you're going to do about Uncle Hiram. You've been
over to Miss Jennieveva's a lot lately, and I don't
think you've been bringing her the laundry either."

Mama laughed and went on ironing Miss Acheson's ruffled petticoat. "It isn't laundry, Callie. It's politics." She winked at me. "Secret politics."

"Won't I ever know, Mama?"

"Indeed you will, but right now the fewer who know the better."

So I waited some more—until the last week in April. Then things really began to move fast. Miss Nellie got married to Mr. Wilcox in our new little church. We all went. The wedding was pretty, even if the bride wasn't. Because we'd had a rainy winter in the desert, plants had really bloomed. For the first time we had flowers for the graves and for weddings. There were bunches of desert dandelions in the church and, for Miss Remington, a big bouquet of white wild daisies. There was one blot on her wedding, though. Uncle Hiram was best man again.

Mama and I sat next to Miss Jennieveva. "Oh, how that sticks in my craw!" I heard her tell Mama.

I didn't know whether she meant somebody else getting married or seeing Uncle Hiram or another schoolteacher going or what. Mama seemed to know, though. "Just you keep your mind on what's happening tomorrow night, Jennieveva, dear. The situation is only temporary."

And still Mama wouldn't tell me what we had in

mind. I didn't know anything about it at six o'clock that next night, but at seven dawn sort of broke. It'd been a funny night. Orrie and Wash had gone up to Stepneys to look at stereopticon views, and Grandpa had gone to the Lion's Den to visit, a thing he didn't do very often.

"Callie, you put on your best dress and good shoes and stockings and get your bonnet, too, the candy-striped ribbon one."

I noticed Mama was getting out her gray silk dress and the new bonnet Pa'd bought her at Miller's for her birthday the first of the month. Even if he wouldn't come home, he remembered our birthdays. Sometimes it was hard to be mad at Pa. Orrie and Wash and I missed him something bad, but we didn't dare tell Mama.

"Where we going, Mama?" I asked her, as I put my sash around my dress.

"We are going to Little Eva's, Callie."

I dropped the sash on the floor. "To a saloon?"

Mama laughed. "No, to the back room."

"What're we going to do there?"

"You and Jennieveva and I, we're appearing before the mayor and council at seven thirty." Mama frowned as she buttoned up her dress. "Tonight we're going to fix Hiram Perkins."

We went around to the back door of the saloon and Little Eva, herself, let us in. "Good evening, Mrs. Perkins and Miss California. My! Don't you both look nice!" she said in that soft slow voice of hers. Then she went on, "The gentlemen and Miss Acheson are already here."

So they were—Mayor Miller and the city council members, Mr. Stepney, the two who were Miss Jennieveva's boarders, and the other two men I didn't know. Miss Jennieveva was all dolled up in dark pink with light pink ruffles on her sleeves and bustle. She had some rouge on and a hat with two white doves in the middle of it. She looked almost good.

All of them were sitting around a big round table in a plain bare room with six cuspidors in it. When we came in, the men got up and bowed and Eph Miller told Mama and me to "take seats." We took the only empty chairs.

Mayor Miller sat down with the others, then cleared his throat, and said, "This is a very serious matter we've come here to consider tonight, the ousting of a member of the school board."

"You're darn tootin' it's serious, Ephraim," broke in Miss Jennieveva.

He gave her a keep-quiet look. "We'll hear your testimony very soon, Jennieveva. Now to relate the

facts of the case." And he told the city council what
Mama and the rest of us suspicioned—that Uncle
Hiram had put the school board up to skullduggery,
and finished by saying, "The fact remains, boys, and
ladies"—he nodded toward the three of us—"that
here we are without a schoolmarm again, even if we
practically have our new schoolhouse built."

"You ought to make Hiram Perkins resign," broke
in Miss Jennieveva again.

"Why?" asked Mr. Stepney. "Everybody on that
board's married by now."

"Out of punishment, that's why." Then she said,
"He put 'em up to it. I know it! He doesn't give a fig
about children's education. He only wants to make
himself popular with the menfolks."

"Besides," Mama added, "the danger might not be
over yet. Hiram is single, remember!"

When I heard this warning, I gasped and almost
giggled. If I wasn't where I was, I would have.
Uncle Hiram's being a bachelor wasn't really dangerous at all, I figured, but they didn't seem to know
it.

"What proof do we have that Hiram Perkins is a
guilty man?" demanded one of Miss Acheson's
boarders. "I don't like to hang a man without a trial,
ladies."

Mama touched my hand. "You stand up and tell them, Callie."

I got nervous and trembly now and my voice shook, but all the same I stood up and repeated what I had heard about aces and queens and what Mr. Cornelius had told Grandpa.

"We'll talk to Cornelius later," said Mr. Miller after I sat down, feeling very grown up.

The other one of Miss Jennieveva's boarders asked, "Why don't we just ask Nash and Metzger and Wilcox?" He laughed. "I guess I forgot the name of the other used-to-be-bachelor on the school board."

"Adams," snapped Miss Acheson. "Benjamin Adams. Don't you dare ask any of those men."

Mayor Miller sounded puzzled. "Why not?"

"Because that'd wreck four homes, that's why. What if their wives found it out?"

"Why would it do that, Jennieveva?"

Miss Acheson looked at Mama and me and just shook her head. I understood, I guessed, what she meant. I'd sure hate to think somebody courted me on the draw of a card because it was his turn and he was that desperate.

Mama explained to the men, and after a while Mr. Miller and the council seemed to understand.

"But you still got to prove the case against Hiram," said one of the councilmen, one of the two I didn't know. "The evidence looks bad against the Duke all right. It don't seem he had the good of Mojaveville's kids in mind so much, but it ain't proved to me yet."

"Well, then, why not ask Hiram, himself—ask him privately?" suggested Mama.

"I will," promised the man. "I sure will!"

Afterward the mayor and council got off onto other things, things that weren't our business, so Miss Jennieveva, Mama, and I went back to the boarding house for coffee and raisin cake.

"Great Heavens, Hope," said Miss Acheson on the way to her house. "Why in the world did you ask that man to ask the Duke if he was guilty?"

Mama laughed. Her laugh was a lot like Orrie's. "Oh, Jennieveva, I've known Hiram for fifteen years. If I'm right about him, and I think I am, he'll brag right out about how he got wives for his friends who wanted them. He'll hang himself out of his own mouth."

The Duke of Kansas did, too. The mayor told Mama at work a couple of days later. Hiram con-fessed just the way Mama had said he would. Eph

Miller sent a message to Miss Jennieveva, who we worked for again every morning. We always did when we didn't have a teacher. The mayor said that he and the council had asked Uncle Hiram to resign from the school board as a disturbing influence and that Hiram was considering the request.

Until April 26 the Duke considered it. Then he fired off a note to the mayor and each member of the city council. It was two words, "I won't."

Mama and Miss Jennieveva, but not me, went back to an emergency meeting that same night at Little Eva's. I waited up until Mama came back home. "What happened? What happened, Mama?"

"Hiram won't resign!" she told me, taking off her gloves. "The mayor and the council can force him but if they do, there'll be a scandal. Everybody in Mojaveville'll know what he did."

"Our teachers too?"

She nodded her head. "Yes, Callie. It won't be pleasant for them. This certainly isn't their fault." She sat down and took off her shoes and sighed. "Callie, there's only one thing left to do, play my ace in the hole. That'll bring the Duke of Kansas to heel."

"What's that?" I asked her.

She closed her eyes. "It's the only thing I can think of that'll save Mojaveville from trouble. The mayor and council don't want to kick Hiram off, and I don't want to force them to, so I'll have to go to work on Hiram. Don't ask me what I'm planning to do. I won't tell anybody that yet—not even Jennie-veva. She's never to know. It ought to work real well. Tomorrow after you get off work at her place, you leave a message at the Lion's Den."

"For Pa?"

"No, for the Duke of Kansas. He's to meet me"—she stopped for a minute thinking—"some place secret. Tell him to meet me in the Reba at noon."

"Maybe he won't come, Mama."

"He will. His curiosity will bring him."

"You sure know how to handle folks, don't you, Mama?"

She laughed and her laugh wasn't funny. "Sure I do—all about folks and how to handle them. Look at this nice place, a crystal palace! It's so odd that your pa likes a hotel better." She waved her hand, with her eyes still closed, around our bottle house. Then she opened one eye and looked at me with it. "All the same, California Perkins, you *will* go to high school—even if it's over my dead body, you'll go and maybe you'll go on to normal school, too." She looked redhead fierce again. "Do you want that, Callie?"

I'd thought hard about this idea ever since I'd

heard Mama had such big ambitions when she was a girl. I knew now that I'd like to be a teacher, too. I didn't want to spend my whole life helping out at a boarding house or getting married right off. I wanted to earn my own way doing what I wanted to do for a while first before I settled down. "Yes, Mama," I told her. "I think maybe I want to."

9 ✳ The Queen of the May

I was a little bit surprised when Mama asked me to come along with her. I thought I'd done my work in front of the mayor and council, but it seemed I had to help her out "fixing Hiram." She and I sat in the Reba with our lit lantern in front of us on the teacher's desk for a half hour before he came.

He was dressed as if he was ready to go out prospecting, and I supposed he had a burro outside waiting for him. "You want to see me, Hope," he asked her.

Mama answered sweet as pie, "Yes, Hiram, I do. I've come to ask you to resign from the school board."

"So you know about that, do you? My answer was 'nope,' " he told her.

Mama kept on being sweet. "Well, Hiram, I think I'll have to convince you then that you ought to quit."

The Duke of Kansas sat down on the edge of the teacher's desk. "How're you gonna' do that, Hope?"

"You're quite a letter writer, aren't you, Hiram?"

"What do you mean?"

"That letter you wrote us in Sacramento about coming up here to the 'tall timber'—that one for instance, Hiram."

"You still holdin' that joshing against me, Hope?"

"I certainly am. I don't believe for one minute that you wrote that as a figure of speech or, as you would say, to fancy up your letter. That was a prac-tical joke, one of the meanest ones I've ever had happen to me."

"You always was a spoilsport," I heard him tell Mama.

"And you, Hiram Perkins, have a mean streak a mile wide!"

"If you got me to come in here to talk to me like that, I'm leavin'." He got up and started out through the tunnel, but Mama called after him.

"I'm not through with you, Hiram! That letter to us isn't the only one I want to take up with you."

Uncle Hiram stopped. "What else is there?"

"A bunch of letters you wrote up in Idaho Territory."

"I wrote lots'a letters up there."

"These were letters to somebody in Portland, Oregon."

I guessed at what Mama meant. I was right. "You didn't sign those letters 'Hiram Perkins,' though. You signed them 'Amanda Appleby.'"

I thought the Duke turned a little greenish when he heard that name. Mama plowed on without mercy. "They went to a Mr. James Cavanaugh, who lived, as I remember, on Burnside Street." Then she asked, "Don't you suppose Mr. Cavanaugh will remember Amanda Appleby?"

"What're you drivin' at, Hope?"

"I suspect it wouldn't be too hard for me to find Mr. Cavanaugh and let him know where Miss Appleby is. Mr. Cavanaugh very well might be still interested enough in her to make a trip down to Mojaveville."

"With his forty-four," I broke in.

"Be quiet, Callie," ordered Mama, while Uncle Hiram turned a dirty look on me.

Then he asked, "What is it you want, Hope?"

"You know very well—for you to resign from the school board. You don't give a hoot about kids getting educated. Some of the rest of us do."

Uncle Hiram thought for a minute, then shook his head. "Oh, all right, if you want to be a spoilsport again," he said. "I never thought you'd turn out to be a blackmailer, too, Hope."

"I always knew you were a practical joker and a meddler in other folks' lives, Hiram. I'm only fighting fire with fire."

That afternoon the Duke of Kansas sent a note to Mayor Miller. It was two words again: "I quit!"

Mama's next project was to get Miss Jennieveva on the school board. On the last day of April Mama called a meeting in the Reba of all the ladies in town—not just the ladies who had kids in school, but all the ladies. Our four ex-teachers were there, too, and so were the Cornish women. Because of the nursing they did during the la grippe troubles, everybody liked them now and nobody dared ever say "Cousin Jenny." Even Little Eva came down out of her saloon to the meeting.

Mama stood behind the teacher's desk and talked. "Ladies of Mojaveville," I heard her say, "you know we have had several teachers this year, but all have fallen into the willing arms of Mojaveville's dashing bachelors. Who could blame them?"

Everybody, even the ex-teachers, laughed.

Then Mama went on easily. "We must admit, though, that now we have no teacher even if the school board says it is trying to get a new one, late as it is in the year. As you all may know, too, there is a vacancy on the school board. What I am about to propose is something extremely unusual—if not unheard of."

You could have heard a pin drop in the mine tunnel. Mama continued, "What I propose is this— to put a woman on the school board to look after the good of our children."

"Huh?" said Mrs. Nanfan. "Huh?"

"Yes," Mama told her, smiling. "A lady, Cunaide. I nominate Miss Jennieveva Acheson for the school board."

"But *you* can't do that, Hope!" put in Mrs. Stepney, looking worried. "Only the mayor and the council can nominate people for that."

"I know I can't, Hattie, but you could manage it. Your husband is on the city council, isn't he?"

I was tickled at the way Mama handled Mrs. Stepney, who was still a mite stuck up, though Belle Ann wasn't at all anymore. Mrs. Stepney frowned, then said, "Well, yes, he is."

"Influence him, Hattie. It's for your children's future welfare."

Mama left Mrs. Stepney nodding, then she spoke to little Mrs. Miller in the back row. "You, Pauline, can influence the mayor."

"I got my ways," agreed Mrs. Miller, and every lady laughed again, even us seventh- and eighth-grade girls standing against the wall.

"And Jennieveva, herself, can influence her two boarders on the city council."

"I'll skimp on the gravy again if I have to," Miss Acheson said, and everybody laughed harder than ever.

"Well," Mama finished, "I trust that next week there'll be an announcement that Miss Acheson has been appointed to the school board to fill Hiram Perkin's unexpired term."

When we walked back home that night, I said to Mama, "It's in the bag, isn't it?"

"Oh, I hope so, Callie," she told me, "but I doubt if your father and grandfather would approve if they knew about all the things I did to remove

Hiram and get Miss Jennieveva appointed. I'm not worried that Hiram or she will tell them, mind you, but I certainly have gone about things in an under-handed way."

"You fought fire with fire, and you won. Miss Jennieveva will be better on the board than Uncle Hiram was."

"I think she will, too, dear, and she says she'll work to get us a different kind of teacher this time. If she gets appointed, she'll influence the school board to send for a special kind of teacher."

"What kind of teacher?"

"The kind that it won't make any difference if the teacher gets married."

"What kind is that?"

"You'll see, Callie. You'll see. But as Mrs. Trewhiddle says, it did take some *schemey louster* to do it."

That was new Cornish to me. "What does that mean?"

"Brainwork, Callie, brainwork."

The next day was May Day and a holiday in Mojaveville. The mines all around shut down, and even the men from the Sequoia came in to town in their mud wagons. They brought Philip Atterbury with

them that day to save Wash the trip, and Mr. Miller
tied the dog up behind his store so he'd be ready to
go out to Mica Gulch with the next day's mail.

There were some big things planned for the day,
a church dinner and the crowning of the queen of
the May, which would have to be Belle Ann or
Gennys or me, because we were the only ones in
Mojaveville close to the right age and unmarried—
even if we were a little bit young.

We didn't know how the day was going to turn
out, though, when we danced in the morning with
ribbons in our hands around the Maypole and
watched the Cornishmen prance in hobby-horse
costumes. That was because Baron Hans von und zu
Upganger hadn't come to Mojaveville yet. He arrived at noon in his magician's wagon. He was quite
a sight, sitting on the seat of his closed-in black
wagon with the words painted in gold and red letters on its sides: *Professor Baron von und zu Upganger Has Appeared Before the Crowned Heads of
Europe.* He had on a high silk hat and a black cloak,
and over his chest was a wide purple band with
medals pinned on it. He had black hair, too, and a
skinny black mustache. We stared hard at him, all
right, but he seemed to like it and stared right back
at us Maypole and hobby-horse dancers.

"What're crowned heads?" Orrie, curious as ever, asked me as the wagon finally rattled past us.

"Kings and queens, and things like that in Europe, I think."

Then the Baron pulled up his team of mules, stood on the seat, and called out, "Ladies and gents, I'll be givin' my show tonight at eight o'clock sharp in yer church. Come one. Come all. Ten cents' admission, one skinny dime, that's all. Come see my magic show, the finest in the world, direct from the shores of Europe."

"He don't talk much like a baron," said Orrie. "He sounds more like Uncle Hiram."

"Oh, he isn't a real baron!" Belle Ann told the three of us Perkinses. "Real barons don't talk like that. Real professors don't either. I met some once in San Francisco at my grandmother's house and heard them talk."

May Day was on a Tuesday night. All the same the old minister from Barstow had stayed over after he delivered our Sunday sermon to be our master of ceremonies. At the church supper I sat across the table from the magician and heard him talk about himself for a whole hour—about himself and all the crowned heads of Europe he'd known and what they'd said to him. Belle Ann kept on kicking me

under the table when he boasted, and Mama kept
giving me warning looks when I couldn't help gig-
gling with Belle Ann.

After the supper Professor von und zu Upganger
started in on his magic show. It turned out to be
mostly sleight of hand, making scarves and things
folks in the audience gave him disappear. Belle Ann
and Gennys and I sat in the front row and watched.
Then Belle Ann whispered to me, "I wouldn't let
him have my cameo brooch, Callie. He'd make it
disappear so well that I'd never see it again."

I knew what she meant. I thought it wasn't very
smart of Miss Jennieveva to give him her jet bead
necklace, but he did give it back finally after the
performance was all over and she had reminded him
about it. Out it came, out of his black hat. Then
after all the clapping had stopped, the Baron held
up his hands for quiet. "Ladies and gents," he hollered out, "I hear tell you're gonna' elect a queen of
the May tonight."

"We sure are!" somebody yelled from the back of
the crowd.

"And I hear you're buildin' a new schoolhouse,
too."

"Yep," said the doctor, who was there in the front
row, too, because Little Eva's was closed while it

was being decorated for the square dance that night. "Even if there isn't a teacher at the moment."

"Buildin' schoolhouses costs a heap of money! Buyin' good books for young 'uns costs money. You folks got plenty of money for extras for the new schoolhouse?"

This question made every adult in the audience laugh, so I guessed there wasn't a lot of tax money.

"Well, folks, I propose to help the new school-house along and to entertain you at the same time. I'll...."

"How?" asked our pa interrupting.

"I'm glad you asked me that, friend," the Baron went on. "Now, who was going to be in charge of selectin' the May queen before I luckily came along."

"The preacher," said Pa.

The Baron looked out over the audience and called out, "Will the Reverend please stand up?" When the preacher did, the magician asked him, "How'd you plan on going about this selectin', preacher?"

"Well, we were going to vote on the young ladies in question by secret ballot just before the square dance started."

"Who are the young ladies? Who are the fair candidates? Read off their names, please, and have 'em stand up and take a bow."

The minister reached into his pocket and hauled out a piece of paper. "Miss Belle Ann Stepney."

"Stand up, girl!" shouted the Baron.

Belle Ann stood up, frowning, then sat down fast while folks still clapped for her.

"Miss Gennys Trewhiddle," read off the preacher.

Gennys got up, blushed, and sat down too, while all of the Cornish miners stamped and whistled.

"Miss California Perkins."

Me, California Perkins, I got up, red to the tops of my ears, and practically fell down into my chair again. I was so embarrassed I didn't hear any clapping. I'd expected to be in the contest because there weren't a lot of choices, but I didn't like the way the Baron was taking it over.

From the platform before the altar the Baron grinned down at the three of us. "Fair as lilies. Fair as roses. Three pure maidens clad in spotless raiment. Flowers of the desert. Roses of Sharon. Lovely as the dawn and young. . . ." He coughed. "Lots younger'n I expected."

Gennys and Belle Ann and I looked at each other. It was true we were all wearing white, each of us with a different colored sash. Belle Ann's was green, mine pale pink, and Gennys' blue. But we didn't think we were fair as lilies or roses or flowers of the desert, and we weren't that young either.

The magician really warmed up after his opening remarks to what he was driving at. "I propose we combine the selectin' of the Mojaveville queen of the May and raisin' funds for a schoolhouse."

"How you going to do that?" Pa asked again.

The Baron held up his hands once more while people began to mutter about what Pa had asked. "By each man voting for the fair maid of his choice."

"We were gonna' do that anyway," came from Pa. "Everybody's vote was going to count."

"You do not seem to get the point, my friend," said the Baron. "Doing things your way no good will accrue to the school at all."

"What's your way, Baron?" asked Mayor Miller.

"It so happens," said the Baron, "I have brought a box of soap, fine imported jasmine-scented soap, from Castile in Spain, up here to Mojaveville today. It is the very soap used by the Infanta, herself. This soap, ladies, will benefit your complexion. It will put roses in your cheeks."

"He's beginning to talk different now," I said to Belle Ann. "This doesn't sound much like Uncle Hiram anymore."

"I think he's memorized some parts of what he says to make them sound elegant, Callie."

"Oh."

On and on the Baron talked about his soap from Spain, then he opened a big box in front of him, one he hadn't used in his magic act. It was filled with cakes and cakes of yellow-colored soap. A smell floated out of it. I sniffed it and coughed. "Is that jasmine, Belle Ann?"

She sniffed, too. "No, I think it's buffalo grease."

And still the Baron went on with his speech, finally coming to the point that with every cake of soap somebody bought from him the buyer got five extra votes beyond the one vote people who didn't buy any soap got. Then he said, "Come on, gentlemen, who'll be the first to buy a cake of soap and win *six* votes for the fair lady of his choice. Ten cents a cake!"

"That's highway robbery," I heard Miss Jennieveva say from behind me.

"Come on, who'll be the first to buy." The Baron was holding up a cake now and waving his arm in the air. He made me feel a little bit sick.

"Not me," said Pa, "I ain't buyin' any soap at all." He got up and left. Mama followed right after him and after a minute so did Orrie and then finally me, blushing again because everybody was staring at

the maybe May queen who was leaving. The Stepneys, Belle Ann, too, were right behind us.

"Well, I never!" exploded Hattie Stepney on the
church porch. "The brass of that man!"

"Where's Washington?" Mama asked Orrie,
who'd been sitting next to him.

"He's still in there, Mama."

"He would be," Mama said. "And he's got ten
cents with him."

We went to Little Eva's then to listen to the two
fiddlers from Barstow tuning up for the square
dances. Belle Ann and I walked over to the May
queen's bower. It was made over an armchair out of
palm-tree branches brought from San Burdoo. In a
basket beside it was her crown, one of real white
roses that'd come from Barstow that morning and
which Miss Jennieveva had made into a crown over
chicken wire. By now the roses were getting a little
brown at the edges, but they still smelled nice, a lot
nicer than the Baron's jasmine soap from Spain.

"I wish that old Baron hadn't come up here and
spoiled everything," I told Belle Ann.

"Yes, I do, too." She looked me in the face. "Callie, do you still want to be May queen?"

I knew the answer right off. "No, I don't think so.
I guess I did for a while, though."

"So did I," she said, sounding angry, "but I don't

want to be anymore either." She pointed to the
crown. "The minister's way of doing things was
right. Now the crown's being bought. Do you know
why your pa was so mad, Callie?"

I shook my head. I didn't really know. Belle Ann
thought she did, though. "That Baron, he'll raise
some money for the schoolhouse and give it to the
Mayor all right, but he'll keep part of it, himself.
My father told me when we walked down here.
That's one of the big reasons why I wouldn't be
May queen for anything—not with that horrible
Baron having a hand in it."

Gennys Trewhiddle turned out to be the queen of
the May and had the crown put on her head—not
by the mayor or the preacher who should have, but
by the Baron. He even led her to her bower and sat
her down in the royal chair. Gennys didn't look very
happy, though, and I noticed how she got up as soon
as she could and put her crown back in the basket.
By this time the square dancing had started so folks
weren't looking at her anymore.

I caught hold of Wash by one elbow as he and
Banjo ran across the saloon floor, trying to see if
they could skid from one end of the wall to the
other. "What happened in there?" I asked my
brother in front of Belle Ann.

"Gennys got elected. The Cousin Jacks, they

bought all the soap—nearly every bar there was. They said they were gonna' wash down mine walls with soap if they had to. Mr. Upganger, he made about forty dollars for the school and about twenty for himself."

"Did you buy any soap?" I asked him. There was a funny smell about him I thought I recognized.

"I sure did." He hauled a cake out of his pocket and showed us. "I got six votes because of it."

"Who'd you vote for?" demanded Orrie, who'd come over to us.

Wash had that sick-cow look on his face as he looked at Belle Ann, so I knew who my own brother had voted for, all right. I guessed I hadn't got even one vote, but I was too mad to care.

Belle Ann and I went up to Gennys soon as we could and congratulated her on being May queen. She had tears in her eyes after we got through, and she told us both, "I'm so glad you aren't mad at me. I hated it, sitting there. It was just awful like, like a horse being sold. My ma, she's mad at my pa and the Boscawens and the Nanfans, too. It was a *wisht* old job a *louster,* it was."

We patted her shoulder, and I said, "It's all right, Gennys. We understand. It wasn't your fault. There wasn't anything you could do about it."

I danced square dances that night with Jenkin

Nanfan and Pa and Mr. Stepney, and the Virginia
reel with Uncle Hiram. He went out of his way to
ask Mama and me and Miss Jennieveva to dance.
Because we were supposed to be ladies, we couldn't
turn him down, but we all three stomped our way
through the dances with him. Miss Jennieveva's
back was like a ramrod when she was his partner,
and Mama's face looked frozen. What I wanted to
do was "put my little foot" right on his big one. I
didn't feel any different later when Wash told me
the Duke had spent five dollars buying soap to vote
for me—even if that was some votes I knew about
for sure.

Orrie heard Wash telling me, and asked, "Callie,
why did Uncle Hiram do that? He don't like soap."

"I don't know, Orrie," I told her. "I don't understand men very well."

When I went to bed that night, though, I guessed
I did understand them a little more. All of us Perkinses went up to Stepneys for a late supper. We
were good friends by now, since the flash flood. It
seemed since the time of la grippe that most people
were better friends—even the Cornishmen and the
American miners. We'd all been in bad trouble together. Even Banjo was my good friend now that I'd

said nice things to him about being a useful Mojave during the flood. I guessed if he'd had ten cents like Wash, he would have bought soap and voted for me.

Mama stayed on to talk about the lending library with Mrs. Stepney, so Pa walked home with Wash and Orrie, who were sleepy, and me. Grandpa was out prospecting again. He'd missed May Day and the Baron. So had Mr. Cornelius.

"Pa," I said, before I went inside, "thank you for not staying when the Baron started peddling soap. Because you got up and left, I got a chance to go, too."

"It turned my stomach, honey. I didn't like to see him makin' money out 'a the selecting of the May queen," he said, after he kissed my sister and brother good night.

"Mama sure agreed with you."

"I figured she would, Callie, if I got up first."

"Do you think the Baron will stay in Mojaveville for long, Pa?"

"Nope." He shook his head in the moonlight. "I think he'll be out 'a here by morning, if he isn't out of here already." He paused for a minute, then he said, "I'm sorry, Callie, that things turned out this way for you tonight. I thought you'd 'a been a

darned pretty queen of the May. I'd 'a bust my but-
tons bein' proud."

"I'm not sorry, Pa. I didn't want to be queen—not
with the Baron running things. Neither did Belle
Ann. We're both sorry for Gennys."

He nodded again. "It wasn't so nice for her, I
suppose. Maybe it was worse winnin'. Well, Callie,
you did learn one thing and that's good—that
there's folks in the world like Mr. Upganger. Not
many of 'em, the Lord be praised. People got to
stand up to men like him—either that or walk out
on 'em cold. Too many people don't see what men
like that are doing until it's too late to stop 'em.
Some of them didn't see tonight that the Baron was
taking over Mojaveville's show from the preacher
and making money out of our May queen where he
didn't have any right to. Folks up here'll get to
thinkin' about it soon, though—if they aren't pon-
derin' it already."

I didn't want to talk about the Baron anymore.
"Pa, aren't you ever coming back to us?" I hated to
see him return to the Lion's Den again.

"Not till your mama asks me!" He tipped his hat
to me like I was a real grown-up lady. " 'Night,
honey. I still think you'd 'a made the prettiest first
May queen Mojaveville ever had." Then he was
gone.

I watched him go down the ledge, and then I
sighed. He was as muleheaded as ever. I wondered
whether I ought to tell Mama what he'd said or not.
She might not like it one little bit, and I could get
into trouble for asking him what I had asked him.

The Baron was gone in the morning just the way
Pa said he'd be. Mama heard that a delegation of
Cornishmen had escorted him down into the desert
at two o'clock in the morning after they'd all been at
the barrel of whiskey in the back of Little Eva's.

I never saw Miss Jennieveva so excited as on the
Saturday after May Day when I went to work at her
place. She was fit to bust as she kept working right
alongside me, dusting and cleaning. "This place has
got to be spic and span—like it never was!"

"Who's coming to visit, Miss Jennieveva—Queen
Victoria?"

"Not to visit—to *live*."

"Who is it?"

"The teacher, Callie, that's who."

I had to yawn while I went on dragging the
feather duster over things. Teachers! How I'd seen
them come and go in Mojaveville!

"We're going to meet the stagecoach from San
Burdoo today at noon, you and me."

This announcement was a surprise. "Me, too?"

"Yes, you, Callie. Because you had something to do with getting Hiram Perkins off the school board, you're going to see *me* represent it—meeting a teacher."

I couldn't help but ask her. "What card did you draw—a high one or a low one?"

She laughed. "Get me my bonnet, Callie. We got to look respectable, so take off your apron."

I went with her mostly out of curiosity to see what kind of teacher it was the school board had hired this time. I figured she could only be a lady a hundred years old.

Well, it wasn't anybody a hundred—not quite a hundred anyway, and it wasn't a lady at all. Miss Jennieveva stepped up and introduced herself to a man. He was nearly as old as Grandpa even if he didn't have a beard or a mustache either. He was tall and skinny with a big eagle beak of a nose, a great big Adam's apple that wobbled up and down, and long yellow hair. He was dressed all in brown checks except for his brown derby, but his vest was yellow. The most interesting thing about him was the gold-painted wicker birdcage in his hand. It had a green and red and yellow parrot in it.

He took off his hat to Miss Acheson, held it over his chest, and bowed. Then I heard his voice. It was different, sort of foreign sounding. "I am Richard Ulick de Vere," he said to her.

"Where are you from?" She sounded suspicious. "I thought you hailed from Frisco?"

"No, dear madam," he told her, still with his hat off. "I am from London, England, only by way of San Francisco." I watched him look around at Mojaveville. Then I saw him smile. I guessed his teeth weren't really his. He breathed deep of our pink-dust air, and said, "Charming! Charming! Ah, how I do appreciate the desert! Egypt! The pyramids—the Sahara, wonderful, wonderful!"

"You been all those places, Mr. de Vere?" Miss Jennieveva asked him, not taking her eyes off him.

"Indeed, madam, indeed I have. There are few places I have not visited, and I do not refer only to the British Empire. Now I can add to my list this remarkable little city of yours."

"You taught school all over the world?" she asked him, not seeming to notice that folks were gathering around them like flies to gawk at him and her and the parrot.

"Oh, no, madam. I refer only to my soldier-of-fortune days!"

"Soldier of fortune? You been *that?*" she said, soft as a mourning dove.

I had to jog her arm a little and point to her

parasol to get her to put it up. It was getting hotter by the minute. She was turning color so fast I was afraid she'd get sunstroke. Then she turned to me and hissed, "Hurry back to my place, Callie. Tell Un Lung I changed my mind. We're having roast chicken tonight and tomorrow, too."

I hurried back. She was sure acting funny. She was going to take Mr. de Vere in as a boarder, parrot and all. If there was any one thing Miss Jennieveva couldn't abide, she told me once when I first started work for her, it was birds!

10 ∗ A Couple of Miracles

"We have to get Pa back home somehow," I said to my sister and brother, when we walked to the Reba the next Monday morning.

Orrie was growing up pretty fast, curious as ever, and turning into a thinker like me, even if some of her ideas weren't much good. "We could all go down to the Lion's Den tonight and stand out in front and roar for Pa to come home with us."

227

"Yep, that'd work," agreed Wash.

"That'd embarrass Mama and Pa, too, more'n anything I can think of," I told them. "We sure can't do that. Everybody in Mojaveville knows that we're a splitup family, but we've been doing it quiet and peaceful so there won't be any caterwauling out in front of the Lion's Den."

"Then what are we going to do, Callie?" asked my sister.

I took a deep breath before I answered her. "Far as I can see, the best thing is to tell Mama that Pa says *she's* got to ask him to come home." I thought for a minute. "She won't like it, but I don't think she'll have to coax him much. He's just about ready to come back, judging from all the eatin' he tries to do here. Just another couple weeks on beans and whiskey, and he'll be ready."

"Why don't we have Grandpa go down and talk to him?" she asked me.

"I don't think it would work. They'd only play checkers. Besides Grandpa's never around anymore. He's always out with old Mr. Cornelius. That's all he thinks about. Grandpa's got silver fever. Sometimes I don't think you can trust old people much!"

"That's true, Callie," Orrie agreed with me. "You can't put a kid's head on old shoulders."

"Right," I told her. Then we didn't talk any more about that problem that day, because we had another thing to talk about—Mr. Richard Ulick de Vere.

I hadn't ever had a teacher like him before, and neither had anybody else—not even Belle Ann with her tutors in San Francisco. "He's got them beat all hollow," she told me at recess that first day. "I think he knows all of Shakespeare and Keats and Shelley by heart. That's because he went to Oxford University."

Well, I didn't know about Oxford University, or even where it was, except probably someplace in England, but it was true Mr. de Vere could recite poems. I guessed we'd learn plenty from him even if he didn't hold much with arithmetic and had worse trouble doing fraction and division problems than I did. We all liked him, though—even Wash and Banjo and the Nanfan boys, although he was mighty elegant for Mojaveville. After all, who else had ever hunted for tigers with a maharajah in India or gone looking for rubies in Burma during his soldier-of-fortune days?

"Is he a crowned head?" Orrie asked me, when we went home that day.

"I don't think so," I told her, "but I'll find out."

"His parrot's named Wellington," she said to Mama that night at suppertime. "Who was he?"

"Wellington was an English duke, Orrie."

"See there, Callie," my silly sister told me, "he's a duke, of course. Even his parrot's one!"

I did ask Miss Jennieveva Saturday, too, while I was doing my work after I fed old Wellington a biscuit and got my finger nipped. She was wearing a brand new dress with blue flowers on it and had on new pearl earbobs. When she talked she sounded funny, as if she was trying to copy Mr. de Vere. "Oh, yes, indeed, California, Mr. de Vere is ennobled. He's a de Vere, ain't he? The de Vere's were the earls of Oxford, you know."

"Is he from Oxford?"

"He most certainly is." Miss Acheson gave Wellington another piece of biscuit. I guessed she liked the parrot, because his cage was out in her parlor, not up in the teacher's room where I thought it ought to be.

"Don't it matter if Mr. de Vere gets married, Miss Jennieveva?"

She shook her head and smiled. "Not one bit, my dear. That only applied to lady teachers."

"I don't think that's fair!"

"Fair or not, it's a school board rule." She flicked her handkerchief at me and nearly knocked me over because it smelled so strong of chypre. "Now go on about your business, child. I must go see to Mr. de Vere's luncheon. Richard has a very delicate stomach. It was all that curry he ate in Bombay that did it."

She was gone, leaving me with her dusty-leafed plant, her feather duster, and the parrot. Wellington gave me a beady-eyed look, a sort of mean look, whistled and said, "Richard! Richard! Poor Richard. My kingdom for a horse!"

Miss Acheson came back soon, grinning. She said to me, "You'll be happy to know, California, that Mr. de Vere will be staying on next year with me. He's promised to help us select books for our lending library. He has all kinds of ideas."

I wasn't too interested in this news, and hearing it made me feel sour. It wouldn't make any difference to me if he stayed on as the teacher because I'd be in high school—if I got to go to school at all. Mojaveville didn't have a high school. Because I felt sour, I said, "I bet you are going to marry Mr. de Vere."

She turned pink as a peony. "Why ever do you say that, California."

"Because you're on the school board, that's why, and it's your turn, isn't it?"

Miss Jennieveva laughed and patted her braid.

There was a bunch of pale blue ribbons on top of it. "Well, dear, as I always did say, miracles do happen!"

I was glad to get out of there at noontime. She was sure giving herself fancy airs that day.

Uncle Hiram surprised us by turning up that night at our bottle house with a basket under his arm. It had a cover on it. "Can I come in, Hope?" he asked Mama, sort of timidly.

"Of course, Hiram. Make yourself welcome. Have some coffee."

"What you got in the basket?" asked Wash. He was still friendly with the Duke. "A present for me?"

"Nope, a present for all of you." He opened it up and inside there was a dog, sound asleep. It was a puppy, a yellow-brown one with long soft fur. "This here's Whiskey," he told us. "I got him in Burdoo for you, because old Philip Atterbury run off."

"Why Hiram, how nice of you. Thank you. Where did you say you found him?" Mama exclaimed, as Orrie grabbed the dog and woke him up.

"In a saloon, like I told you, in Burdoo. They'd already named him. He knows his name so don't you go tryin' to change it. Maybe old Whiskey can catch pack rats for you. I heard tell from Gid you got troubles with rats."

Mama looked down at her shoes. "Not anymore, Hiram." Then she asked, "What are you doing these days?"

"Nothin' much," he answered. "Some prospectin' some days; other days workin' in the Queen of Hearts when I feel like it. Nothin' special, Hope." He looked around him. "Where's Grandpa Thompson?"

"Out prospectin'," Wash answered for her. "He ain't hardly ever home no more."

"Well, it keeps him and old Cornelius happy, don't it, and out of trouble?" The Duke of Kansas laughed. "He might even surprise you by strikin' it rich. After all, I done it once. Miracles do happen."

"Hey, that's just what Miss Jennieveva said to me yesterday," I came out with.

"About *what* miracle?" asked Mama, pouring more coffee. She had a warning look on her face, and I knew that she meant I shouldn't mention the school-board funny business and the man in Portland with the cocked forty-four and all that sort of thing.

Wishing I hadn't said anything, I white lied so fast I amazed myself. "About her getting to like birds." Then before they could get a good look at my face I bent my head down and started to pet Whiskey.

A real miracle did happen the third week in May. We couldn't believe it until the man at the assay office told Mama it was true—every word of it. Grandpa and Mr. Cornelius struck it silver-rich out in the same area where the flash flood came down.

There was one thing funny, though, about Grandpa. He didn't seem very happy or very excited either. Instead, he seemed sort of down at the mouth and just mumbled "thanks" when Pa and Uncle Hiram and a lot of other folks came up to our house to congratulate him.

"What's botherin' you, Grandpa?" I asked him two days after he came home. He was peckish, hardly eating at all.

"It's Cornelius, Callie. Out there after we made our strike and posted our notices that the property was ours and started back with our burros, he confessed it to me."

Wash lifted up his head and listened, too. He was sitting across the table trying to get Grandpa interested in a checkers game, but he wouldn't play.

"What? Wasn't Mr. Cornelius at Shiloh?" I knew Grandpa put a lot of stock in his being in that battle with him.

Grandpa sure sounded sad. "He was, Callie. He was, but he and me, we was on diff'rent sides. He was a Confed'rate."

"Oh, my!"

"He ain't even from West Virginia, honey, him and Little Eva. They're from *Virginia!* He was deceivin' me all along, and he's six months older'n me, not six months younger. That makes him the oldest man at Shiloh, and on the wrong side, too."

I put my hand on his shoulder. "Don't take it to heart, Grandpa. The Civil War's been over for nearly twenty years." Then I had a bright thought. "You were both in the Mexican War, weren't you, and you were both on the same side then?"

He looked up at me. "Well, I suppose we was at that, Callie."

"That's the thing to think about, Grandpa. You can talk about that war with him instead of the Civil War."

Wash said, "You're rich, Grandpa, you got two wars!"

We didn't say anything more about it, but that night Grandpa combed his hair and beard and changed his clothes and went up to Little Eva's for the first time since he and Mr. Cornelius and their burros had come up out of the Mojave.

The next day he and Cornelius met with Mr. Stepney and sold their mine to him, the mine they'd named the Veracruz after a Mexican War battle they were both in. Grandpa was a rich man now. He asked Mama to quit work at Miller's but she wouldn't.

"No, Father," I heard her tell him, when they thought I'd be asleep. "I have to keep my self-respect in front of Gideon."

"I don't understand you, honey. I got plenty of money to take care of you and him and the kids, too. I lived off Gid for years because of my rheumatism."

"That doesn't mean we're going to live off you, Father. Gideon wouldn't do that." Mama sounded proud when she spoke about Pa.

They were still arguing when I went to sleep.

Wash got passed by Mr. de Vere into the fifth grade and Orrie into the sixth. Next fall they'd move out of the cool Reba into the hot new schoolhouse, but I wouldn't. Along with Belle Ann, who was a couple grades ahead of her age because she'd had tutors, Gennys and I got passed all the way out of the Mojaveville school.

It made me sad. Gennys was going to high school in San Bernardino, where she would board with a Cornish family, in the fall. Belle Ann was going to school lots farther away, back up to her grand-mother's in San Francisco. But what was I going to do?

Mr. de Vere offered to teach me privately Saturday afternoons, but I didn't take to that idea much.
That way I'd need eight years at least to get
through high school.

"I want to be a teacher someday, too, like my
mother wanted to be," I complained to him.

"A commendable choice, California," he told me,
"very commendable. I believe you would make an
excellent teacher. You are possessed of remarkable
patience and you have a fine sense of humor."

"But what'll I do now, Mr. de Vere? Thank you
for offering to tutor me, but that'd take years,
wouldn't it?" I guessed maybe I wanted to go to
high school more than I would have naturally, because I didn't see how I was going to get there.

"It probably would at that." He leaned back in his
chair, and said to me, "I think you'd better take this
up with your parents. Perhaps they would send you
to board in San Bernardino also—as Miss Trewhiddle is doing."

I only shook my head. I didn't see how I could go
away as long as Pa and Mama were split up. Grandpa's being rich didn't seem to make things any better than they had been since we came to Mojaveville over a year ago. Even if we owned a team of
chestnuts and what I guessed was the fanciest two-

seater buggy in San Bernardino County, I couldn't see that we were much happier.

I took up our troubles again with Wash and Orrie. They hadn't forgotten one bit what Pa had said to me May Day night.

"You just got to tell Mama," came from Orrie.

"How come it has to be me?"

Wash was on Orrie's side. "Because you're the biggest and the oldest and you're the one he talked to. Besides you're the one who's ready for high school."

"You look! High school hasn't got a thing to do with Pa coming back home to live." I was beginning to feel selfish about what I wanted when what we all really wanted most was not to be a split-up fam-ily anymore. Then I said something that sounded bolder than I felt. "I'll talk to Mama tonight after supper."

"We'll back you up," Wash offered, just as bold.

"No, Wash. There isn't any call for you to get in trouble, too. He didn't talk to *you*. If she thinks one of us is a quitter when it comes to Pa, let her think it's me."

"All right, Callie, but if you need us, you just yell," Wash said. "We'll come runnin' and tell Mama it's our idea, too, and not all your fault because you're askin' her."

"What I'm doing, you know, is asking her to swal-low her pride, that's what," I explained to them. "That could stick in anybody's craw. It'd stick in mine if I was her."

"But you ain't got the three of us kids to look after," Orrie put in.

That night our beans and corn-bread supper was a quiet one. Nobody talked much. Mama didn't seem too tired after she soaked her feet, but she didn't seem much interested in a two-handed game of cards with me after the others had gone to bed either.

"You have something on your mind, don't you, Callie?" she asked me all of a sudden, while I was trying to get up my nerve to tell her.

I hesitated, then I remembered I was supposed to be bold. "Yes, Mama, I do."

"Is it about high school?" she asked, calm as could be.

"Sort of—in a way."

"You want to go away and board, Callie? Father says he'll send you. I'd take money from him for that."

"I don't want to go! Not away from you and Grandpa and Wash and Orrie—and Pa!" I burst out with.

"No?"

"No, I don't. I won't go alone."

"You don't want to be a teacher?"

"I didn't say that! I don't want to go away from you. If I have to go anywhere, I want us all to go."

"Then you'd leave your pa behind up here?"

"No, I said *all* of us!" I leaned across the table toward her. "Mama, I had a talk with Pa the night that horrible old Baron magician was up here in Mojaveville. Pa's ready to come back to us. I asked him to come home."

She got up, went to the stove, and poured us both a cup of coffee, but didn't bring the sugar and canned milk over with her. "Is he now, Callie?"

"He sure is. He hates it at the Lion's Den. He's sick of whiskey and beans for breakfast. He's really ready to come home."

"Then why doesn't he?"

Her question was what I'd been waiting for and what I was scared of, but I answered all the same. "Pa says *you* got to ask him!"

She didn't say a thing except, "Have some coffee, Callie. If you're old enough to stick your nose in your parents' affairs, you're old enough to drink it black."

I drank it and it was terrible, black as Miss Acheson's jet jewelry. Mama boiled it a long time to get it the way she liked it.

"So you think I ought to give up my pride?" asked Mama, eyeing me over the rim of her cup.

"Yes'm," I told her. "He's stubborner than you. I guess ladies just have to give in more'n men do."

"Who told you to say that to me? Jennieveva?"

"Nobody." And that was true. It's what I'd figured out myself.

Mama got up, took off her apron, then put on her bonnet. "Where do you think I'm going, Callie?"

"Down to the Lion's Den?" I said, hoping.

"And what do you think I'm going to do there?"

"Ask Pa to come home."

Mama nodded, not smiling. "Well, that's *part* of what I plan to say to your father. But there's one other thing you better know. I'll take him back on one condition only—that we *all* leave Mojaveville together. How does that suit you?"

"It suits me fine, Mama."

"Well, you'd better know this then, too, Callie. If he won't come, then I'll go to the county seat and make this separation legal."

I knew what she meant all right and that was a terrible thing. I didn't say a word and I couldn't blame her for what she was thinking, but it was still a terrible thing. She opened the door, went out, and slammed it shut, leaving me sitting at the table alone with a half-full cup of black coffee in front of

me. I knew I'd better finish it off before she got
back, so I choked it down.

By the time I'd downed the last awful gulp, Wash
and Orrie had come in, sleepy looking. Wash had the
puppy, Whiskey, in his arms because the dog slept
with him. Mama's slamming the door made them
wake up.

"Where's Mama?" Orrie asked. "Where's
Grandpa?"

"Grandpa's down with Mr. Cornelius. Mama went
down to the Lion's Den." Then I looked around at
our bottle house, our stove and shelves, and almost
said, "I think maybe we're going to get out of Mojaveville," but I didn't. I knew they wanted Pa back,
but they might not want to leave Mojaveville the
way Mama and I did. I didn't have the strength to
listen to Wash tell me how much he'd miss Banjo, or
Orrie wail to me about Columba, her best friend.
After all, I couldn't tell them how much I'd be missing. I wouldn't be missing much, not when Gennys
and Belle Ann were going away anyway.

"Oh, let's go to bed," I told them after a half hour
had gone by. "They're arguing down there. It could
take all night. If Mama catches you two up, she'll
skin you alive."

But it didn't take all night. I was in bed trying to

sleep, but because of the black coffee couldn't, when I heard them come in—first Mama's footsteps, followed by Pa's heavy ones. Then I saw the glow of the kerosene lantern I'd turned down grow yellower as somebody turned it up. Then came the scraping sound of the granite coffeepot being put on a still-warm part of the stove. I knew what it meant. Pa had come home for good.

A week later, the first part of June, we left Mojaveville. Grandpa drove his buggy with the three of us ladies inside it. All of our furniture and other stuff in Slum Gullion Slim's mud wagon followed behind. Pa and Wash and Whiskey rode out into the desert heat in Slim's wagon, too, because that's where they chose to be.

"I'm gonna' leave this camp the same way I come in," Pa told us the night before we left.

"Me, too," agreed Wash.

"Not me," came from Grandpa Thompson. "I'm too old for buckboards." Then off he went to say good-by to Mr. Cornelius.

Pa and Mama had decided we'd live in southern California—either in San Burdoo or in Riverside, where our Christmas oranges had come from. We'd look over both places and make up our minds before

we settled down in any place. "The greenest, prettiest one, with water somewhere nearby, is going to
win with me," Mama told me privately.

Folks were nice to us before we left. The Nanfans
and Trewhiddles baked pasties for us to eat out in
the desert and Gennys said she'd see me a lot if we
decided on Burdoo. Belle Ann gave me a beautiful
purple and blue and gold Chinese parasol to remember her by and a kiss. Banjo gave Wash an
ocarina and Miss Jennieveva presented Orrie and
me with silver-mounted hairbrushes and Wash a
derby hat like Banjo's. She cried when we left and
made Mama promise faithfully to spend Christmas
of 1883 and 1884 with her and Richard and Wellington. We did promise.

Mama said, "Jennieveva, I can't thank you
enough for all the things you did for me and my
family. We do have lots of things to remember,
don't we?"

The reminder made Miss Acheson smile. She still
smiled when Mama went on, "I can't think of anything nicer than a December holiday in Mojaveville.
Just ask us anytime between November and March,
and we'll come visit you."

"And between April and October, we will come
see you. Now you keep in touch, you hear." She put
her handkerchief to her face, I saw Mr. de Vere put

his arm around her so she wouldn't stumble up her front steps.

"What'd she mean by we?" Orrie wanted to know.

"Them—her and Richard. She can save her money now and not go up to Frisco. I think maybe she and Mr. de Vere have a understanding," I said.

"What's that, Callie?"

"If you can't figure it out, you're too young to know, Orrie."

When we went by Miller's, we had our biggest surprise of all. There was Uncle Hiram, sweeping the porch. He was wearing a long white apron and had a pencil behind his ear. He was taking Mama's place as a clerk.

Mama had Grandpa pull up the horses. "Hiram!" she exclaimed, when he came over to the side of the buggy. "I thought you were going to be foreman of the Veracruz mine?"

"Nope, I didn't want that job, Hope. This way I get to see more folks, not just miners, and I'll hear what's goin' on in town instead of bein' stuck all the time out in the Mojave. I didn't want to make up mine payrolls. That's responsible work and I don't add too good."

"So is clerkin' responsible work, and you got to add a lot in the job," Grandpa scolded him.

"I know it. I know it, but I got customers who'll

be inter'sted in helpin' me tote up their bills right, don't I?" He grinned. "Besides I don't know how long I'll be stickin' with this job neither. My foot's still pretty itchy, folks. If I can strike it rich once and you can strike it rich once, Grandpa, maybe I can do it again!" Hiram stuck out his hand and we all shook it. "Come visit us folks up here in the desert some of these days," he told us ladies.

"We will," Mama promised him. "When we get settled, we'll write you a letter." She thought for a minute, laughed, and said to him, "Just don't you get any ideas about answering it. I don't think I'll ever believe a word you say again. And I don't think you'll be with Mr. Miller long either. You'll never change, Hiram Perkins. You're incorrigible!"

"Oh, I've changed a lot already," he told her with a wink. "I don't think I'll write letters no more. I'll take up readin' books now that I hear the lendin' lib'ry's startin' up next month."

"Please do that, Hiram. It's less dangerous than writing letters." Mama laughed again, then tapped Grandpa on the shoulder to go on.

Grandpa's buggy was ahead of Slim Neuberger's wagon. We started down the ledge first while Pa and Wash said "good-by" to the Duke of Kansas, too. I sat in the back seat with Mama while Orrie sat up front with Grandpa. We didn't say a word as we went down the steep slope. I turned my head, though, to look at the cemetery. Then, I remembered lots of things, things I knew I wouldn't ever forget about our year in Mojaveville.

The desert lay ahead of us, bright gray-white in the summer sun with here and there dots of greenish bushes. On two sides of us, north and west, were the mountains, gray-blue ones with a little bit of snow still on their tops. After I'd looked my fill at them because they were so beautiful, I stuck my head out the side of our buggy and looked back toward Mojaveville through the cloud of dust we made.

Yes, there was a mud wagon following us.

"Pa, he's coming right behind," I said to Mama.

* Author's Note

During the 1880's the Mojave (pronounced *Mo-hav-é* to rhyme with *slav*) Desert area of southern California was one of the state's largest silver producers, a position it held until the early 1890's when the price of silver dropped, and the boom in the desert was over. Today the Mojave is noted for its production of borax.

There were quite a few towns in the desert in the

period of this story, towns that flourished for a time and that today exist as very small communities or as ghost towns. My "Mojaveville" is a composite of these towns of the 80's.

If the town I have written of is fictional, other matters are not. My description of 1882 San Bernardino is an accurate one. Fish Ponds existed; my oasis, Bass Ponds, is patterned after it.

Many of the incidents described here are true incidents. The mail-carrying dog is a historical figure, featured in lore of the Mojave. The robust tale of the marrying schoolmarms is also a true one. People did live in bottle houses and were happy to find them because they were cooler than ordinary ones. May Day was actually an important holiday in early-day San Bernardino County; May queens were chosen with much pomp. One camp at least truly celebrated April Fool's Day by shooting up a dummy.

My remarks about the Cornish miners are also true to life. "Cousin Jack" and "Cousin Jenny" were fighting terms, much resented by the Cornishmen and their wives. My Cornish speech is, although very strange, the true Cornish way of talking. Part of the research for this novel was done in England. There I found these examples of Cornish talk. The one-line sentence of Gennys and Columba's grand-father is actual Cornish language, a language that passed out of usage in the nineteenth century in the British Isles. Trewhiddle, Boscawen, and Nanfan are genuine Cornish names.

An actual epidemic of la grippe (or perhaps influenza) struck one of the Mojave camps in the summer of 1882. The doctor who dealt with it drank a lot, but unlike my Dr. Aubrey, was finally run out of town.

Wyatt Earp is connected closely with the history of San Bernardino County after he left Tombstone, Arizona. As a matter of fact, for a time in his later years he lived in San Bernardino. Earp was a frequent visitor to Mojave mining camps, and it is true that he was greatly beloved by the children. I have no real notion why except for the glamour that surrounded him, but to make it more concrete, I have made him free with small change.

Flash floods are commonplace in the Mojave. It is the true mark of the tenderfoot to sleep in the middle of a gully. No more dangerous thing can be done. Today it is not at all unknown for a desert flash flood to catch an automobile and its unwary passengers. Afterward no trace of either car or people can be found. The Santa Ana dust storms I describe are the bane of southern California living, not only in the desert but in irrigated areas surrounding it, places such as Riverside and San Bernardino. They are cruel, parching winds which fray nerves, kill plants, and out in the desert can blast the paint off an automobile with the sand they blow.

Life in the Mojave Desert was not easy in pioneer times. I have my Perkins family depart the desert. Many others did not, however.

The desert has rewards and lures of its own—as many desert dwellers today insist.

In writing this particular novel I used many and varied sources—books, pamphlets, magazine articles featuring pioneer reminiscences, and newspapers of the day. Four sources were of major value— the *San Bernardino Times* of 1882-1883; the *History of San Bernardino and Riverside Counties* by John Brown, Jr., and James Boyd; Remi Naudeau's *Ghost Towns and Mining Camps of California*; and *Ingersoll's Century Annals of San Bernardino County 1769 to 1904.*

I would like to express my gratitude to the reference librarians of both the San Bernardino and Riverside Public Libraries, who found material for me in many places I would not have thought to look and who, by their interest and enthusiasm, heartened me in my work investigating this difficult and sparse field of local history.

Patricia Beatty
Riverside, California

August 1967

About the author

Patricia Beatty, now a resident of Riverside, California, was born in Portland, Oregon. She was graduated from Reed College in Portland, and then taught high-school English and history for four years. She later held a position as a science and technical librarian, and then worked as a member of the technical information staff of the explosives department of the Du Pont Company.

Mrs. Beatty has lived in Coeur d'Alene, Idaho; London, England; and Wilmington, Delaware; as well as on the West Coast. Her husband, Dr. John Beatty, is an Associate Professor at the University of California, and they have a daughter, Ann Alexandra, born in 1957.